The
Afterdeath

David Lewis Paget

BARR BOOKS

For Christopher
Because you appreciated the humour.

ISBN – 978-0-9750856-8-4

Chapter One

Jonathon Pepper sat in his office on the other side of Port Waterdale, and buried his head in his books. He was a grim, austere man of 66, and by rights he should have retired by now, but he found it impossible to disentangle himself from the business that his great-great-grandfather had started while it remained in such a sorry state. His son Edmund didn't have the drive required to pull it out of the doldrums, and it would take a lot more than an energetic approach to do any good now. What was needed was flair.

The sign over the door read 'Ebenezer Pepper & Sons, Funeral Directors, Est. 1867.' In those days, you only had to throw a shingle up and you were in business. Ebenezer hadn't even owned a spade in 1867, but there was nobody else in the town that wanted to do the job, so he fell into a vacant niche and stayed there. His sons Albert and Henry had nothing better to do during those first few years, so they joined him in the venture. Henry eventually moved away to go prospecting, and Albert took over when his father turned eighty in 1879.

There were plenty of funerals in those days, especially of small children. Those that diphtheria didn't dispose of, scarlet fever did. They buried them in rows, without any headstones, and the tiny mounds they made may be seen to this day.

Albert plodded along until 1915, and then handed over to his son Arthur, who continued the tradition until 1951 when he keeled over with a heart attack in his 71st year. Benjamin, Arthur's 45 year old son continued the business up until 1970, when Jonathon took over at the age of 35. He had hoped that Edmund would follow in his footsteps in the year 2000, but Edmund was a little slow in growing up.

Edmund had been born in the 'summer of love', 1967, and to look at him you'd think that the hippie generation had stamped its impression on his person from day one. In clear opposition to his father he had decided to grow his hair shoulder length, which was nevertheless tied back on funeral days with a black ribbon. The rest of the time it blew free, and he complimented it with an Indian shirt, jeans and Indian beads that he wore in clusters around his neck. He spent his spare time wooing the local wenches, though he had no heart for extended relationships.

At work, however, he was quite the opposite. He had studied embalming, and would prepare the bodies for burial to look as if they were ready for another fifty years of life. He left the make-up to Brindy Somers from the town, who worked part-time in a beauty parlour, and the rest of the time slaving over the body of some old harridan, trying to give her in death what nature had denied in life.

On this particular day Jonathon summoned his son to a family conference, and Edmund turned up dressed as the proverbial gypsy. Jonathon looked up at him from his own neat and subdued suit, and sighed. 'I do wish that you would treat this firm seriously, Edmund. We are the inheritors of a proud family tradition. The least you could do would be to dress appropriately during the firm's time.'

'Okay Pop. Though I do remind you that as it's my day off. I wouldn't normally be here.'

'That's as it may be, Edmund. However, if things don't turn around, you will normally 'not be here' anyway, as the firm will have collapsed. Do you understand that?'

Edmund fell into a chair. It was not so much news to him - he had heard his father sounding off about critical business conditions on a hundred occasions. But this time there was something in his father's tone that indicated things might be worse than suspected.

'Just how bad is it,' he said.

'Well, according to my figures, we are already running in the red. Unless the township is hit by a sudden plague, which is unlikely, we won't be able to hold out more than six months, at the very most. I'm afraid that 'Valhalla' has stricken us to the core.'

Edmund stood up and walked over to the window. From where he stood he could see across the cemetery to the long, gaunt building which had taken away a large slice of their business.

'It casts a long shadow at this time of day, doesn't it,' he said.

'It casts a long shadow into our future. Why on earth the council allowed them to go ahead with it is beyond me. If I'd suggested it, they'd have come down on me like a ton of bricks,' said Jonathon, irritably.

'As usual, what the Great Hall wants, the Great Hall gets. It's always been the way around here, Pop. Well, what do you suggest we do about it - advertise?'

'That's not the answer. We already advertise, and it makes no difference. People of this generation are obviously looking for something a little different. It's not good enough to be buried anymore, or just plain cremated. They want to put their parents on show. There's a creeping unreality about the way most people deal with death today, like an avoidance of the main issue.'

'I can't say 'He's dead, madam,' I have to say 'He passed away', 'He has gone to a better place', 'He is beyond the realm of mortal man', and other such poppycock! People don't accept death today, they shy away from it. The world lives in denial.'

'Well, if that's your feeling, then maybe we'd better come up with something to out-Valhalla Valhalla. Do you want to build a mausoleum on this side of the cemetery?'

'No! - No buildings. We have to outsmart them, not copy them. Besides which, we wouldn't have access to the sort of funds that built that monstrosity. No, we have to think smart, and think quick, by God! Put your thinking cap on and come up with an idea that will allow our internments to pop up out of the ground to meet their relatives, and I think you'll have it licked.'

Edmund thought for a minute.

'Well.... we have the expertise as far as embalming goes, so our corpses won't deteriorate. They could be put on show, dressed in their contemporary finery. What about taped messages to their descendants - you know, push a button and great aunt Bertha will talk to you, that sort of thing.'

'You're moving along the right track. Work out a way for the corpse to stick their head up and wave, or do something that they were good at in life. In this age of great technology there has to be a way. It's just a question of harnessing it.'

'I think I know who to approach. He's a few threads short of a blanket, but I believe he's a real whiz at anything computerised. I suppose we could offer him a royalty.'

'If it's good enough, we could franchise it out, don't worry,' said Jonathon.

Edmund went off deep in thought, while Jonathon went back to his books.

II

Eugenia Barry packed a basket with home-made pickles and jams, and headed off along the dirt path that ran alongside the cemetery. Off among the trees she could see the roof of the little ramshackle church that had been patched up and re-commissioned for the Flower of the Flock. It had been a Wesleyan Methodist Church at one time, but had been left to deteriorate once the new church was built in the town during the 1920's. The old church had been left to rot, to be overgrown with weeds as sheep and dogs made it a temporary home in inclement weather. Then Pastor Adam Cain had appeared in the district, proclaiming that the way to everlasting life was to purge the flesh of its sinful desires by exorcising them from the body. The only way to do this was to wear the flesh out by overexposing it to indignity and exhaustion.

Cain was a thirty-two year old opportunist and con man, who also doubled as a sex addict. Three or four times a day was not unusual for him, and he speculated that he must have been at the head of the queue when they were handing out hormones. Age, colour or creed, it was inconsequential to him as long as it was female, accommodating and satisfied his needs of the moment.

He was far from being a romantic, however. Sex to him was a cold, hard business which saw the woman relegated to the object of his desires, the key erotic element being his ability to bend and shape her to suit his needs. As a result he never became carried away while indulging his lusts, but remained apart from the emotional element of the act, watching as if from a distance as the woman opened up to him, and offered herself for his gratification. On climax he would break out in a cold perspiration which seemed to emanate from his brain, and spread chillingly down his back. A large part of his desire was tied up with his total control of the situation, and of his partner of the moment.

He discovered the old church and moved in, living in a well-sheltered corner of it while he cleaned it out and patched the roof to make it cosier. Then he partitioned off a section for his living requirements, and put out a sign welcoming new adherents to become members of the 'Flower of the Flock'. At first only a curious few turned up, and the majority of these didn't return. But as time went on pastor Adam seemed to collect a hard core of adherents who were as fascinated as he was in this theory of sinful desires, and they kept returning, to learn more about it, more actually, about how to purge themselves correctly.

Eugenia Barry, at 54, was as concerned to purge her desires correctly as the average thirty-year-old. As pastor Adam said, it's not how old you are, but what you do, how often, and with whom. An older person necessarily had more stored-up desire to dispose of than a younger person, so it was necessary to work on it without delay. He said it would be a tragedy if you died only partially freed of your fleshly longings, as you would then have to come back and do it all over again.

Central to the pastor's philosophy was the place of woman in the scheme of things. As the very source of lust itself, women carried a very heavy burden into the next life, unless they made serious amends in this.

'It is women who paint their lips and nails, women who accentuate their eyes with make-up, and women who perfume themselves in order to seduce unsuspecting males. It is women who drape themselves with revealing garments, designed to suggest an accessibility that has lured many a man into a mistaken approach. It is women who tease and flirt, and accentuate the eroticism of their bodies to snare the male. It is therefore woman's responsibility to relieve men of their desires, and in doing so, purge themselves of their own lust!'

That meant, said Pastor Adam, that the women should make themselves available to male members of the Flock at a moment's notice, so that a sinful desire could be dispelled immediately in a way that only a woman could. Woman, the source of lust, thus becomes woman, the dispenser of virtue!

Eugenia Barry had been impressed. She had plenty of fleshly desires remaining, even though she was 54, and her husband was beyond being of use to her in that respect. She had applied to become a member of the Flock at the last meeting, and Pastor Adam had been most charming. He'd pointed out that it was important that he have a private interview with her before she began the ceremonials with the other members of the Flock. This was where she was headed now, for a one-on-one with the pastor.

Once inside the church he locked the old oaken doors, saying that he wouldn't brook any interruption during his ceremonial interviews. He was young, only thirty-two, and possessed a powerful body, which Eugenia looked at with pleasure. He led her through into his living quarters where there was a jolly fire burning in a grate. He had fashioned a chimney out through the wall, and it worked well enough, the smoke from the fire being drawn outside the building without too much of a draught being felt in the room.

'It is important that I establish your fitness to become one of the Flock,' he began. 'You do understand that out of every twelve applicants, only one is acceptable in this exclusive order?'

She felt a ripple of excitement pass through her. 'I've... I've brought you some small gifts, nothing much,' she added in a rush. 'I pickle my own and make my own jams.'

'...And most appreciated, I'm sure,' said the pastor, without the hint of a smile. 'There is nothing like the treasure of God's food, prepared by the hands of a good woman.'

Eugenia caught at her breath, his face was close to hers.

He moved back, and she relaxed.

'Now to the matter of import, Eugenia. I'm sure that you have a basic understanding of why I asked you to see me alone, for this first instance, anyway.'

'Yes, yes, I...' Eugenia couldn't get it out. She was overwhelmed by his eyes.

Chapter Two

Augusta Branwood's eyes snapped open the moment the blind went up. Her jaw started moving exactly half a second later.

'Four years three months two weeks and five days... I get another day! Do you hear that, my girl?' she said to Joanne Destry, who was attending to the other blinds in the room.

Joanne didn't answer. She knew from long experience that an answer was not required to that particular question.

The old lady sat up in bed, or 'snapped into an upright position' would be a more acute description. Every movement Augusta Branwood made was positive, sharp, and designed to conserve energy. She believed that three score years and ten marked the end of natural expectations, and that every day over that biblical figure was a plus.

'My father used to say that the only two things you couldn't avoid in life were death and sex. These were the only inevitabilities. When I grew older, I told him that he meant death and taxes, and d'you know what he said?'

'No - what did he say?' said Joanne, politely.

'He said that you could always avoid taxes!'
The old lady let out a throaty cackle, swung her legs over the side of the bed and propelled herself onto the floor in one bound.

'But he was right about the sex!'

Joanne smiled to herself. The old lady was feisty.

Augusta stood there in a short nightie, showing off a pair of legs that would have looked good on a woman half her age. She threw a sheer robe around herself that hid nothing and made a charge for the door, Joanne fetching up in the rear. She flung the door open and burst out onto a landing, protected on one side with an ornate white railing which ran unchecked for fifty metres until it met the top of the central stairway leading down into the hall.

'Where's that damned stud of mine? I only keep him on so I can work up a good appetite in the morning.

'Wi...lll....iam!' she yelled, calling for her personal physician Dr. William Laurens, who was noticeably absent that morning. 'He's probably out chasing those damned tourists - I hope he shoots them!' she said, shrilly, as she careered on down the stairs.

'Damned impertinence,' she snapped. 'Wanting to look over the Great Hall, would you believe... as if we were open to the public,' she declaimed to one and all.

'Out of the way, Agnes, I'm on a mission,' she yelled at the doddering figure of her cousin, Agnes Coverleigh, who shrank back against the banister as she charged past.

'Saddle up the horse, Frederick,' she yelled at the butler, 'I'm going for a gallop!'

Augusta continued her mad charge through a doorway into a downstairs toilet. Joanne stopped and waited outside. She would be in there for five minutes at least, and then off again.

The butler sidled off quietly through another door, and as he opened it Joanne caught sight of the giant rocking horse sitting waiting in the middle of the room. She suppressed a smile and looked the other way, watching Agnes as she made her shuffling way towards the breakfast room. By the time Augusta got there, Agnes would have wolfed down most of the toast.

Augusta presently came storming out of the toilet, heading for the romper room.

'Time for a brisk gallop, my girl, get the juices flowing, work up an appetite. I've told Agnes that's what she's missing out on, a bit of good old-fashioned manual stimulation, but she's so morbid! No wonder she's got no life in her.'

They crashed through the door and Augusta headed straight for the horse. Frederick the butler had meanwhile adjusted the saddle and stirrups, and was waiting patiently to give his mistress a boost up on to the horse's back. She got her foot in the stirrup, threw her leg over and lowered herself gingerly into the saddle.

His job done, Frederick retired circumspectly to the hall, and shut the door behind him. Augusta waited until the door closed.

'Let's go for a gallop!' she roared, once she had made herself comfortable.

Joanne walked over to the horse and turned a switch on its chest. A motor cut in and the rocking horse sprang into an instant gallop. Augusta let out a couple of swift 'whoops', and then settled down to ride it.

'This was my late husband's idea,' she shouted above the motor. 'He said that it might be able to keep me satisfied, because he couldn't.' She laughed, and then experienced a minor palpitation, and gasped 'Canter, canter!'

Joanne turned the switch to canter, and the horse took up a different rhythm.

'You should (whoop) give this a try (hmmmph) yourself young lady. Get yourself ready for (oo wwooo) a real, er, m-man.'

Augusta waved a hand and Joanne turned the horse off. Augusta rested on the horse's mane for a minute, then hoisted herself off.

'Ooh! Weak in the knees! I'll be all right. Let's to breakfast.'

The old lady charged out of the room, her white hair sticking up at all crazy angles, and headed for the breakfast room. As they stormed through the door, Agnes snatched the last piece of toast out of the rack, and hurriedly buttered it.

'You're a gannet, Agnes, a veritable gannet! Order some more toast, Miss Destry, and tell the cook we'll have some fresh coffee too.... and don't think you're having any, either, Agnes. You can finish off that pot. I see you've already scoffed enough breakfast for three.'

'But Augusta, I've had so little to eat lately, my health has been shattered as you know. I didn't think you'd mind if I built myself up a little.'

'The last thing you need Agnes, is building up. What you need is a good rogering from some young stud. You're 58 Agnes, not 74. I'm the ancient one around here, and I could screw you under the table, Agnes!'

Agnes threw up her hands, and shuddered.

'Must you, cousin? Your language... reeeeaallly!'

'What - Screw? Stuff and nonsense, Agnes. A woman needs a good screw to keep her fit and healthy, you should know that. But you don't, do you? You'd rather lie in that coffin of yours, waiting to die, playing the Lady of Shalott.'

'Really, Augusta!'

'Don't deny it, Agnes, I've seen you. Lying in that damned silly coffin of yours...'

'I was in my private room, Augusta. I really think...'

'There is no private room in the Great Hall, Agnes, you should know that. As long as I'm alive, there will be no private rooms, either. Ah, here comes the coffee and toast. Miss Destry, you sit down with me, and don't let Agnes touch our toast and coffee. She's had enough, haven't you Agnes?'

'Well, I must say,' said Agnes, but what she was going to say was immediately ignored. She excused herself and shuffled off, muttering to herself something about dignity, poor taste and wounded feelings.

II

The Coverleigh Estate, or Branwood, to give it its modern name, was the focal point of a thousand-acre estate, ranged around what was known locally as 'The Great Hall', which had been founded by Sir Jeremy Coverleigh in 1862. His wealth originated from sheep, and he became a great investor in mining and railways.

The adjacent town of Port Waterdale had grown up around the early shipping and farming, and until the 1930's the area had been a hive of activity. Then the shipping dropped off, moved to a deeper port fifty miles away, and the last mine closed, leaving the area to farming and small business.

The town dwindled from 18,000 at its peak, to fewer than 8,000, and the pace of life slowed. Much of the population were thirty plus, and a lot ranged from late forties to late sixties. It was becoming a retirement area, a last outpost for the baby boomer generation.

The town cemetery was central to the interaction between the town and the Great Hall, because old Sir Jeremy's original acreage included the land that eventually became the eastern end of the cemetery, while the western end was situated on crown land. As a result, the town lay on one side of the cemetery, the Great Hall on the other.

The significance of this had not been noted until recent years, when young James Coverleigh, heir to the estate, had decided that it wasn't much use owning a cemetery, or even part of one, if you couldn't make money out of it. He was desperately short of cash, always, as Augusta kept the family on a short purse-string. She made allowances for James - (even though she despised him for his Spanish looks) – and for her cousin Agnes Coverleigh, and she kept servants. But there was not the huge disposable fortune that the family had enjoyed in the past, so efforts had to be made to secure further income.

When James approached Augusta with the idea of adopting a modern approach to burial, Augusta was inclined to listen. She was not so insular that she didn't realize the world was changing, and that unless the old landed families adapted they would go under.

Jimmy's idea was that instead of wasting what little ground there was left by selling off the remaining land as individual plots, they should build a vast mausoleum, capable of housing literally hundreds of cadavers, on shelves rising as high as the roof, and the length of the building. The storage cost would be minimal, there would be a wall for cremations, and whole families could be housed together so to speak.

Augusta thought it would be a marvellous idea for the peasants to have something similar to the wealthier family's vaults, which had been a good source of revenue in the past.

People today were less inclined to build such large marble tombs; the cost had become prohibitive. Not only that, but families were not such tight-knit groups as they used to be, and there was less sentimentality. Today everyone looked at cost first, and one enterprising company in another state was even putting together cardboard coffins for the destitute. In such a climate, a fast food mentality would not be out of place in the burial business, and Augusta grudgingly gave James her blessing to go ahead with the scheme.

With Augusta's verbal backing, the bank manager was happy to loan the money required to build the mausoleum, and by calling in many favours from the past, and squeezing tradesmen to the limit, a most impressive building was erected in no time at all.

It was two hundred yards long, and stood forty-five feet high, with gothic columns moodily guarding the entrance. This was in the centre of one long wall, and consisted of two huge wooden doors rising to a peak in the centre, above which, on the roof, were mounted two massive Viking horns. Beneath these, in lettering large enough to be seen three hundred yards away was the word 'Valhalla'.

Reaction amongst the population of Port Waterdale was mixed. There were those who considered it a monstrosity, and resented having to look at this monument to death every day of their lives, and there were others who were fascinated with the concept. Once complete, James began to give a series of guided tours through the building, and the fascination increased.

The colour scheme of the interior had been especially chosen to give the building atmosphere. Starting off with black on the left, it gradually emerged through red, orange, yellow, grey, pale blue, to white on the right. This, of course, made one end of the building a lot darker than the other, which fairly glowed. There were no windows at all, but solar powered lighting was recessed into hidden alcoves, so that it cast shadows and light in strange flickering patterns on the walls.

Shelving was built in, seven levels in all, and access to the various layers was via a walkway which circled the entire building. In the middle of the red wall, in huge black lettering, picked out with curling yellow flames was the word 'HELL'. To enter it, one turned left at the main entrance, and passed through a portal of artificial flames, guarded by devilish denizens with long tails and tridents.

In the centre of the building, at the initial entry point, the colour faded into grey and the word 'PURGATORY' dominated the section. Finally as the pale blue faded into white, grey lettering with black highlights picked out the word 'HEAVEN'. To enter here one had to pass from 'PURGATORY' through gleaming gates studded with pearls. At the far end of this section there was a group of plaster angels, ten feet high, looking benignly down on the visitors, and one held a harp. As was demonstrated, and to the crowd's delight, this angel not only held the harp, it also played it. At the touch of a button its mechanical arm sprang into action and picked out 'Jesu, Joy of Man's Desiring'. As it finished, everyone applauded.

'Is that the only song it plays?' said one woman, sniffing. 'Because if it is, you'd get mighty sick of listening to that throughout eternity.'

'No indeed, madam. This particular model, the Gabriel, is pre-programmed with twenty-one psalms and forty-five Anglican hymns, twelve Wesleyan hymns, and five Christmas carols. You'd have to be here a long time before you heard them all. It is all designed, as you can see, to give a heavenly atmosphere to those who require a strictly moral and uplifting Afterdeath. For a small fee, there is an arrangement whereby your coffin lid is automatically lifted twice a day, or at those times when Gabriel is playing your favourite tunes. It's like having a box seat at the opera, and not just a season ticket, either. This is for Death!'

'Wouldn't that be unhygienic,' said a man in tweeds, with thick spectacles.

'Not at all. Each cadaver will have been properly embalmed before being interred, so there will be no putrefaction at all. You will look as you looked in life. In fact, you will look so good that your relatives will be able to visit you from time to time, and they will be able to open the coffin to introduce you to your great-great-grandchildren. We are looking at a new concept in death. We like to say that we are at last bringing death to life.'

The group turned and made its way back through 'PURGATORY'. Here there were no angels, and the grey background made the atmosphere appear dreary. In the middle was a huge metronome, ticking away regularly and monotonously, and at each side of the hall was a huge pair of balances, straining first one way, then the other, but never quite going out of balance.

'As you can see, ladies and gentlemen, we are now in 'PURGATORY'. This was where our lord suffered for three days before ascending into heaven. This is where we wait to be cleansed of our sins in this life. The larger the sins, the longer the stay. All our cadavers spend at least a week in 'PURGATORY' before being moved along, either to heaven's abode, or to the depths of hell, where the entertainment is more of a popular kind. This way, please!'

'HELL' was the most interesting and lively section of the hall. Along the sides poker machines continually spun their apples and oranges, their Jacks and Kings in a never-ending cacophony of gambling fever. A jukebox sprang into life occasionally, playing old rock and roll records such as 'Great Balls of Fire!' and 'Highway to Hell'. A radio spat out football scores, and a number of television screens re-ran 'Dallas' over and over again for all the bored housewives. Other sets ran 'The Young and the Restless', re-runs of 'I Love Lucy' and endless documentaries on Aardvarks and Aboriginal culture.

'This section, of course, was designed to be either great fun, or the most mind-deadening, boring and repetitive bedlam that we could devise - according to your taste, of course. This is where the element of choice comes in. The peace and platitudes of Heaven, or the garish, lively, sinful domain of Hell!'

'We are entering a new age, ladies and gentlemen. The days of dumping a cadaver into a hole in the ground, and then forgetting about it, are coming to an end. There is no reason why a well preserved cadaver may not have many years of interesting, new experiences, if interred in 'Valhalla'.

'Think about it. Reflect on what you would want for your loved one – indeed, for yourself. You owe it to yourselves to plan for your own Afterdeath, not leave it up to the vagaries of some ancient deity to decide it for you. Here at 'Valhalla', you can do just that!'

Chapter Three

From a distance the Great Hall was quite imposing. A large central house of two stories with an impressive entrance hall and staircase did for Augusta, her cousin, and the live-in staff, while a single storey North and South wing stretched away from the house on either side. The North wing was inhabited by James Coverleigh, heir to the estate, while the South wing was closed off and left to fend for itself against the forces of nature.

Up close the neglect of the South wing could be seen more clearly, the paint peeling, shutters hanging off – where they hadn't already succumbed to the force of gravity – and windows covered in grime. Somewhere behind that crumbling façade was a ballroom that had once witnessed gaiety and splendour in the passing parade. But it had not rung to the sound of laughter and music for almost forty years.

The central house had fared better, with an imposing circular driveway bounded by flower beds, still tended by a part-time gardener. The windows still sparkled, but in the early mornings were hooded, like eyes with the lids half-closed.

The blinds were always pulled down at night, and released early the following morning as if to announce that the building was now awake, and ready to greet the day.

James Coverleigh was the only heir to the estate, courtesy of the fact that Augusta had never managed to produce a son or daughter of her own. Much to her disgust, she realized that when she went, there was no alternative but to see ownership pass to the 'other' side of the family; back to the Coverleigh's in fact.

Nothing galled her more than this point, because James was descended from a Spanish grandmother, Maria Alvarez, and had inherited her olive skin, black hair and rather cunning countenance. What's more, he was short, only 5'6" – not like the Branwoods who tended to hover around the 6' mark. Everything about James tended to rub Augusta up the wrong way, and he in turn despised her arrogance and overbearing attitude to the rest of the family.

'Jimmy Spick' was Augusta's private nickname for him, and sensitive to his colouring as he was, this used to enrage him. He insisted on being addressed as 'James', as if this would underline the Anglo-Saxon side of his origins.

Anyone who called him Jimmy was either corrected or ignored.

On the wall of his room he kept a family tree to which he referred every day of his life. It was a source of bitterness to him that when Randolph Coverleigh, the incumbent, disappeared in unusual circumstances in 1928, it was Randolph's sister Eliza who inherited, rather than his grandfather Raymond. Of course Raymond was only eleven at the time and grew up to be a poor sort of fish, marrying a devious Spaniard who not only dominated him with her tempers and tantrums, but bore him a son who looked more like a Romany Gypsy than a Coverleigh. This was James's father, Gordon, a simple man who had camped outdoors most of his life, roaming over the estate and leaving behind tell-tale signs of his camp-fires, and the half-eaten remains of the wildlife he cooked on them.

There was no way Augusta was going to leave the estate to Gordon, and she had elaborate plans for breaking it up and selling it off if it looked like going in that direction. But Gordon had succumbed to pneumonia three years before at the age of 59, so the way was clear for James to inherit.

'Well.... At least he tries to behave like a civilized member of the family,' Augusta remarked, grudgingly. 'He wears a suit and shoes, which is more than his father did.'

James looked at the wall chart each evening on his return to the North Wing, the details burnt on his brain.

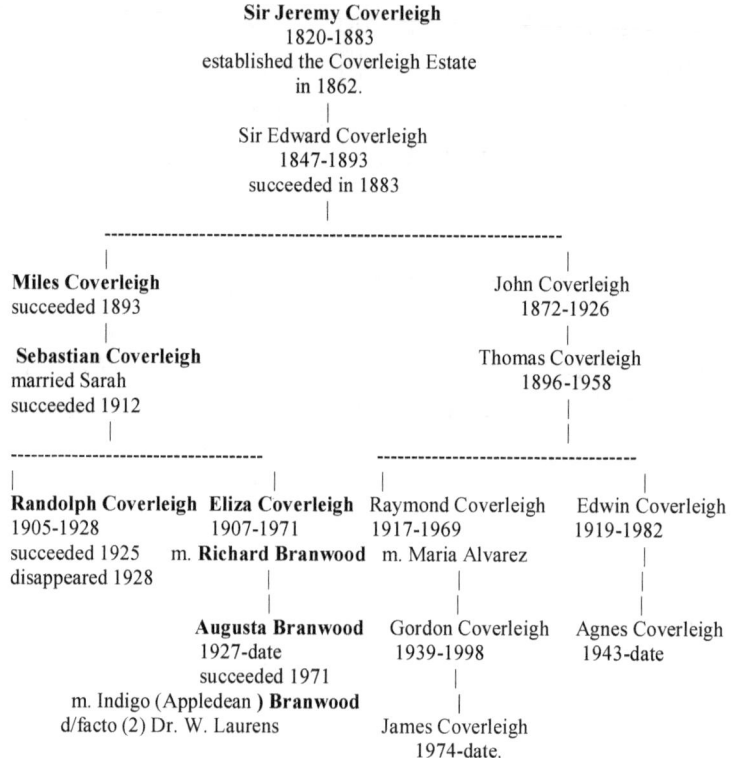

Sir Jeremy Coverleigh
1820-1883
established the Coverleigh Estate
in 1862.
|
Sir Edward Coverleigh
1847-1893
succeeded in 1883
|

Miles Coverleigh
succeeded 1893
|
Sebastian Coverleigh
married Sarah
succeeded 1912
|

John Coverleigh
1872-1926
|
Thomas Coverleigh
1896-1958
|

Randolph Coverleigh   **Eliza Coverleigh**   Raymond Coverleigh   Edwin Coverleigh
1905-1928   1907-1971   1917-1969   1919-1982
succeeded 1925   m. **Richard Branwood**   m. Maria Alvarez |
disappeared 1928 | | |

Augusta Branwood   Gordon Coverleigh   Agnes Coverleigh
1927-date   1939-1998   1943-date
succeeded 1971 |
m. Indigo (Appledean) **Branwood**
d/facto (2) Dr. W. Laurens   James Coverleigh
                               1974-date.

James took great comfort from the chart. It meant that one day, all this would be his. No more going on bended knee for Augusta's handouts! No more humiliation! It was little wonder that he had, from time to time, contemplated various ways of getting rid of her.

II

Dr. William Laurens was taking the sun in a well-hidden alcove around behind the North Wing. In his hand was half a bottle of Jim Beam, the only breakfast he ever took.

He took another swig, and thanked god that he had been able to vacate the Great Hall in time to avoid Augusta's daily summons.

'Shilly Bitch!' he slurred, blinking into the sun. 'Flucking nymphomane... mane...iac!' he stuttered, as the word eluded him.

It was not uncommon to see him drunk before nine o'clock in the morning, especially when he was caught, and had to perform for the mistress of the house.

Dr. Laurens and Augusta went back a long way, long before that idiot Indigo Appledean had arrived on the scene, and married her.

In the early days he'd had quite a crush on Augusta, and had hoped that one day he would be able to pluck up the courage to ask her to be his bride. But each time the opportunity presented itself, Laurens had got cold feet, and waffled on at such length and to such dismal effect, that Augusta had given up on the subject. Then he would take himself off, ranting and cursing for being so inadequate, and throw a few double bourbons down to settle his nerves. By the time he'd finally made his mind up for a last minute do-or-die effort, Indigo was firmly in the driving seat, and Dr. William Laurens was relegated to the pantry.

For the next few years, Laurens had made himself useful in the local hospital, at the same time acquiring a dependency on cocaine that saw him almost disbarred. Realising he was in trouble, Augusta came to the rescue, and appointed him as her personal physician; just about the time of that debacle over Indigo. What a foul-up that was!

Laurens grinned to himself, and took another swig. The balance of power had changed after that. She had something on him, no doubt, but now he had something on her as well, and he never let her forget it.

With Indigo safely out of the way, the two guilty secrets merged, and Laurens began sleeping with Augusta at last. She was 41 by then, and he just ten years younger. Now he was 64, and his libido was definitely lacking. Years of alcohol abuse had taken its toll, and he now ran and hid every time he heard that mating call.

Two or three times a week he straightened himself out, quit drinking for a day, and called in at the hospital to keep his hand in. The work was not demanding, just tedious. However, it ensured that he kept his license to practice, and gave him a bit of extra money to indulge his habits.

He had hoped that Augusta would settle an amount of money on him to enable him to become independent. He thought she had over $600,000 invested in various stocks and shares, and another $200,000 plus to keep on top of family expenses. But she was thrifty, and there wasn't a dollar spent that she didn't know about.

During their lovemaking bouts, he had often lain back afterwards and asked her what provision she had made for him, should she not survive him. Finally she had told him that he would be provided for, never fear, as she had no intention of that little foreigner James inheriting the lot. But she wouldn't be more specific. He had to be satisfied with that.

III

When Eugenia Barry got home, still flushed from her experience with the Pastor, she found her husband in the bedroom trying to hang himself. This was not an unusual happening; he usually did it three or four times a week, whenever the pain in his neck and back became too much to bear. By stretching his spinal cord, he was afforded considerable relief, for a day or two at least. Then the pain would return and he would get the rope out.

'Hello dear,' she said, as she breezed through the house. 'Lovely day outside. You should go outside and get some fresh air, you look a bit peaky.'

Reginald rotated at the end of the rope, trying to gasp out a reply as his face turned blue. 'Gerrrarrrgh, ddeeaarrr. I aaargh...'

He gave up, put his feet back on the chair and stood up.

'I was trying to say, dear, that this exercise has the most unexpected side effects. Besides fixing my back up, I get the most incredible erections. Look at this! Do you feel like a game of ride the wild horsey?'

Eugenia looked doubtfully at his pride and joy. It was so long since it had stood up for him that she thought it would be a waste to let it go. But would it stay up?

'Very well, Reginald. Get down and you can have five minutes with Lucy, but five minutes only. Then I have to peel the spuds for tea.'

After puffing and panting for a good two minutes, he had to admit defeat.

'Blast it! I'm going to have to get one of those suction pumps and a rubber band,' he said. 'I read all about them in the Senior Citz. Yearbook.'

'Well, get off me, Reginald. I'm running behind as it is. When you've got it all worked out just give me a hoi.'

Eugenia went back into the kitchen and washed her hands, while Reg went back to his neck stretching exercises. It had to be faced, Reginald was long past his use-by date. At 68 he'd been no good in that department for years.

She was annoyed somehow, and then she noticed that he'd taken her favourite chair from the kitchen, and was using it to stand on in the bedroom. This was too much! She put the kettle on, and then stood looking out of the window, towards the cemetery, and that little old church on the far side. Pastor Adam Cain had turned out to be well built in areas other than his shoulders. She gave a little shiver as she recollected those moments in the old church, the delicious feeling of being an abandoned woman.

She hoped Reginald wouldn't get in the way of all that. As a husband, he would probably cut up rough if he discovered that his wife was going to be rogered by half the congregation at the church. He might even try to forbid it.

She tapped her fingers on the vinyl surface by the sink. That was a terrible thought! He might spoil everything for her, just as she was about to put matters right in her life after ten years of enforced celibacy. On the other hand, if he insisted on attempting to mount her all the time, and failed, that would be a frustration in itself, and might even undo the work the Pastor was trying to accomplish. She listened to him bumbling about in the bedroom, and made a sudden decision.

Reginald was swinging from the rope again when she walked back into the bedroom. He was making little choking noises, and she ignored him as she snatched the chair out from under him.

'Really, Reginald, you'll have to find another chair to use. I need this back in the kitchen.'

She paused in the doorway, looked back at him hanging there, an agonized look on his face. 'I'm just going to have a cup of tea. Come in when you're ready.'

Reginald twirled on the rope, desperately hanging on to it to try and relief the pressure on his neck, but he was choking, nevertheless. He attempted to cry out, but all the sound he could make was a weak croak, and he suddenly became aware of a movement in his nether regions. By the time Eugenia came back into the room, seven or eight minutes later, Reginald was just about done for. His alter ego was not, however. No-one was more surprised than Eugenia. She'd thought he was dead!

He began to wriggle on the end of the rope, so she sighed, grabbed him around the legs and with an effort hoisted him up about two feet, which instantly took the pressure of the rope from his neck. He began to revive, rather too quickly she thought.

'Oh thank God, my dear. I thought you were going to let me die!'

'I am,' she replied, and dropped him abruptly, the two foot drop being just enough to break his neck.

IV

Werner von Keppler was busy at his computer when Edmund Pepper called in to consult him about the family problem. His room was a clutter of electronics journals, inventors' magazines and UFO data, printed out from the Internet and scattered haphazardly across the room.

There were anti-globalisation posters on the walls uttering dire threats should the world's corporations continue on their sorry binge, and others slamming corporate America as the modern Satan. Werner himself was a grey-haired eccentric who rarely left these four walls, yet he was in contact with organizations across the world, most of which had either an anarchistic bent, or a nihilistic philosophy.

There was no moderation in Werner's world. His idea of voting was to set fire to his ballot paper before shoving it hastily into the ballot box - (for which he'd served twelve months at one of Her Majesty's Prisons) - or to write obscene things next to the names of the election hopefuls.

'Harold the goat', 'Jenny the spotted frog', 'Bernard the pig-dog fascist bum-sucker!' None of these were sheeted home to him, because the scrutineers had no idea who it was.

When Edmund walked in, unannounced, Werner leapt from his chair, hastily shoved a sheet of scribbled notes into his mouth and attempted to swallow it whole, yelling: 'It vasn't me, I don't know anyt'ing about zis - ya!'

He stood with his hands in the air for ten seconds while he scrutinized his visitor through his pebble lenses, then slowly lowered his arms.

'Donner unt Blitzen! You haf come for zuh milk money? I told zem in zuh shop I vould be in next T'ursday.' Then he pulled what remained of his notes out of his mouth, and attempted to straighten them out. They were beyond repair.

Edmund tried to placate him.

'I'm sorry, I gave you a shock. When no one answered the door I thought I'd just stick my head in and call out. I guess you didn't hear me.'

'Too vuckin' right I didn't hear you! I nearly shitted my pants,' said Werner, annoyed. 'You haf just destroyed t'ree hours uf research on zuh manufacture of zuh mercury svitch. So vuck it! Vat do you vant?'

'I came here for your help,' said Edmund. 'I know you're a bit of an inventor, and I was hoping that you could come up with a solution to our problem. You see, we're the local undertakers, and we've come up against some unfair competition that's sending us to the wall.'

'Valhalla!' Werner spat out. 'Ze capitalist pig-dogs of deaff. Zis corporate way of doing t'ings is turning into a plague. I haf seen zis Valhalla, zis monstrosity! First t'ees corporations take ofer our lifes, zen zey take ofer our deaffs. A man cannot die in peas any more. He gets shoved on zuh shelf, tventy feet in zuh air. Gott in Himmel!'

'Well that's just the point, see. If we are going to be able to continue to offer people ordinary burials, we have to stay in business. If we go, then no one will have any choice in the matter. But a lot of people these days want something different, and unless we can offer them something that appeals more than Valhalla, we've had it.'

Werner peered at him through his lenses, comprehending the problem.

'Vat did you haf in mind?'

Edmund took a deep breath. This wasn't going to be easy.

'What we need - for those people who would otherwise go to Valhalla, of course, not everyone - is 'pop-up' coffins, preferably see-through. A long oblong box of perspex, which would be buried with the cadaver standing up. We could arrange all that, wiring of joints etcetera, so they wouldn't sag. Then, dressed in their contemporary clothes, and properly embalmed, they could rise up out of the ground to greet their descendants. We haven't worked out the details yet, but maybe a taped message that would play a greeting. We could record that before death in most cases. We'd like to call them 'Pepper's Pop-ups.''

Edmund looked at Werner in apprehension. There was no knowing how he'd take this. Maybe he'd throw him out.

'I see! And who would haf access to zees 'pop-ups'?'

'Oh - only relatives. We could lock them down with a key, and only make the key available to the actual descendants of the person concerned.'

Werner nodded. 'And vat about headstones?'

'We were thinking that these could be fashioned out of pressed steel, and mounted on the 'roof' of the coffin. That way, the pop-up takes the headstone up with it, and saves a lot of space as well.'

'Ingenious! I like it,' said Werner, grinning broadly. 'But zere must be some t'inks about condensation. A heater and fan at zuh bottom to dry inside zuh perspex. Und to drive it up, a 12 volt D.C. Motor, high torque. A car starter motor vould do zuh trick. Vould zees bodies deteriorate?'

'Not once we've embalmed them. They'll still be looking good after 200 years as long as they're sealed in.'

'Zo - a vacuum, huh? Ya! Leave it vit' me, I vil vurk on zuh design t'is afternoon. You vill have it tonight. Who vill make zees?'

'We were thinking the local engineer. We'll take out a patent, of course, and you will receive royalties. We suggest a partnership, you, myself, and my father, Jonathon Pepper.'

'It sounds gutt to me! Ve vill shake on it.'

They shook, and Edmund left, feeling that at least they had a chance.

V

Brindy Somers was visibly upset when she came out from seeing Dr. Carstairs. He had tried

44

to break it to her gently, but the x-rays didn't lie. She had an inoperable tumour on the cerebral cortex. An optimistic estimate would give her three months. At 27 years of age, this was not the sort of thing Brindy either wanted to hear, or would easily accept. She burst into tears at the news, and Dr. Carstairs had dropped his professional manner to put his arm around her, and comfort her. The fact that he had been taking her out for the past six months didn't usually conflict with their professional relationship. When she had called to see him on medical matters, he had always remained very correct. This time, it was different.

Brindy was a strikingly good-looking woman, with long blonde curls, blue eyes and pale, translucent skin. She had a dimple in each cheek, which enhanced her smile, and a beauty spot at the corner of her mouth. Her body was magnificent, with firm breasts and a trim waist, broadening out below to taper off in a finely muscled pair of legs. To look at her you would think that she had the world at her feet. She was a highly skilled make-up artist, very much in demand by both funeral parlours, and highly paid for her work. But a problem with her vision, and recurring headaches had driven her to seek professional advice, and the answer was that it was already too late.

Richard Carstairs, as he was known when he wasn't doctoring, was thirty-eight. He had allowed any number of opportunities to slip past him in previous years, with any number of assistants, nurses and receptionists. But lately he had felt the need to settle down, to make a proper home for himself, to marry and have children. His work had thrown him into contact with Brindy at the mortuary, and he had admired her from afar. When he finally asked her out she was flattered that a doctor would be so interested in a mere make-up artist, and said yes. It might have gone all the way, except for a little thing called a tumour.

'I'll stand by you, always,' he had said gallantly, when breaking the news.

'Do you mean at the funeral?' she replied, bitterly, and ran out into the night.

'I'm not gonna die, I'm not gonna die,' she insisted to herself, as she made her way home. This was not the way her story should be ending, on a slab, waiting to be made up by whoever took her place at the mortuary. It couldn't happen to her.

'God! - How can you do this to me? My life is just beginning,' she wept. She got angry and stormed around the house, smashing things that she had lovingly saved up for in previous years. She ran out into the rain and turned her face skywards, letting the raindrops sting her face and soak her hair. She was *alive*, she *felt*, she grieved her own imminent demise.

'Fuck you!' she screamed at the heavens. 'Fuck you! Fuck you! I'm not ready to die!'

But deep in her heart she knew it was true, unless she could find a wonder cure - maybe herbs, maybe drugs. Surely there was something.... Why was it inoperable?

'I'll get another opinion,' she thought. 'Richard doesn't know everything – he's not a specialist, after all. I'll go to the top. The top man! It's going to be all right! This is a nightmare, and I'm going to wake up soon... Oh, God! I'm going to die!'

That morning she had been called in to Valhalla to make up a young girl who had taken an overdose. Elspeth Valentine, just eighteen, so young and vulnerable. She had lain there on the slab looking as if she had fallen into a deep sleep, and would wake again when a fairy prince kissed her on her unsullied lips. But she was deathly white, and she had that wax-like skin that said *'corpse' – 'death' – 'there is no inhabitant in this body'*.

Brindy had looked at her and felt compassion, something that she rarely felt. It wasn't often that you got the young ones, and the old ones, well, they had lived their lives. She was so inured to the dead that she rarely looked at them with anything but a professional eye. They were just dead.

The difference between them, and the clients in the beauty parlour, was that they didn't expect a conversation with the make-over. They were totally pliant, dependent on your sure touch to get them looking just right. They wouldn't complain if you got it wrong, they just waited with eternal patience for the rituals to be completed, and the final resting-place to be chosen. They were very undemanding clients.

Now she was to join them. Brindy Somers, 27 years of age! Not quite as innocent as Elspeth Valentine, but nor was she as ready as Elspeth had been to take that last journey, either. For Elspeth, for whatever reason, had taken her own life! Brindy was to have hers taken from her. It was a different thing altogether.

Chapter Four

Joanne Destry finished off her chores for the day, and prepared for her afternoon off. She left by the servants' door at the rear of the Great Hall, bidding a cheery farewell to the cook, and saying she'd be back that evening. Once outside, she checked to make sure she wasn't being watched, then ducked around the side and made for the disused South wing.

There was a lot of undergrowth around the base of the walls, covering what had been a large car park in the 1930's, but there was now nothing but neglect. She made her way around to what had been the old laundry in those days, pulled open the decaying screen door and pushed on the main door. It gave easily. This was her usual means of entrance as the lock had rotted off the door some years before.

As far as she knew, she was the only one who ever visited this part of the old building, as to all intents and purposes it had been abandoned for practical use since the 1960's. She made her way through the laundry and out into a passageway, dusty and cobweb ridden.

The third door on the right held the remains of what had been the great library, though that had last been in use during the time of Augusta's great-grandfather, Miles Coverleigh. He had been a scholar, and had collected works of distinction from all over the world, having little else to do except count his money.

As an adjunct to this he had also imported rare volumes of period pornography, including erotic Chinese etchings, the notorious works of de Sade, the writings of Aleister Crowley including his Book of Magick, and a whole selection of black and white Victorian photographs of unashamed London prostitutes who supplemented their incomes by posing for contemporary photographers of the time, such as the Earl of Innesvel, and Baron Bolger. Central to this collection was a lengthy manuscript detailing the weekly happenings at the Hell-Fire Club, with eyebrow raising descriptions of titled rakes in their favourite environment, including the Earl of Sandwich.

None of this section had been removed when the library was re-located to the Great Hall itself, and Joanne had spent many hours poring over the contents of this unique collection. She was fascinated with this evidence that the Victorians had been pure by reputation alone, and that the actual facts were that they had been a bawdy people, delighting in the sins of the flesh, whilst upholding a strictly moral and religious facade for the benefit of the lower classes.

But there were other works, which engaged Joanne's attention even more. These were historical volumes, many of them dealing with the history of the Coverleigh Estate, now known as Branwood. Sir Jeremy Coverleigh figured largely in these histories, as did his son and heir, Sir Edward Coverleigh. These forerunners took the history almost through to the turn of the century, when the Right Honourable Miles Coverleigh inherited in 1893.

Miles had only one son and heir, Sebastian, who was by all accounts rather an eccentric character who delighted in sleeping out of doors, in all weather, with his flock of sheep. The sheep were still important to the Coverleigh Estate in those days, though it was not generally considered appropriate for the master of the house to take such an interest in the day to day maintenance of the flock.

Sebastian married a farmer's daughter, who was unlettered in the extreme, and who was of such a simple disposition that she would run through the house, naked, pretending to be a moo-cow. Sebastian often joined in these crazy gambols, though he preferred it when she pretended to be a lamb, and bleated. The servants would lock all the outer doors at these times, and deny all visitors, though the stories still got out to the township about the 'goings-on' at the Great Hall. Somehow in all these doings, Sebastian's wife, Sarah, managed to get herself pregnant and delivered a son, Randolph. This was in 1905. Two years later she delivered a daughter, Eliza, and it was around these two that the family fortunes took a mysterious turn.

In 1923 Sarah had somehow fallen into the sty while feeding the pigs, and had been eaten, all except her pigskin shoes. The only reason the family knew that she was gone was that her feet were still in them.

Sebastian was committed in 1925, after being observed cavorting around the countryside in shepherd's garb, buggering the sheep. He was quietly slipped into a padded cell at Forest Hill Sanatorium, and forgotten about.

Life at Coverleigh continued as per usual, with Randolph now in charge at the tender age of twenty. Eliza and he had never got on, and now that there was no parental influence in the house the pair squabbled incessantly.

Eliza began to court a young man called Richard Branwood, the son of a Pitt Street Lawyer and a Kings Cross stripper, whose short liaison made the stripper a great deal of money. She was happy to ditch her unwanted offspring on to the Lawyer in return for a small cottage and three thousand pounds.

Richard was sent to the country to be brought up by the managers of his father's property, and he was educated at the best schools money could buy. He only ever met his father twice, once when he graduated from college, and once on his father's deathbed, when he discovered he was to inherit 1.3 million pounds. He was already married to Eliza by this time, and living in penury at Coverleigh Estate, cordially despised by Eliza's brother, Randolph. They had taken over the South Wing of the house, and tried to avoid Randolph as much as possible.

Randolph kept himself to the Great Hall and the North Wing, and had a succession of girlfriends who left him the moment they realized he was barking mad. Some of Sebastian's taint had rubbed off on Randolph, though he tended to admire larger animals than sheep, and was often to be seen riding across the estate on his favourite mare. He would seek a high point of the estate, pull up the horse, cry out something that sounded like: "Yoicks! Yoicks! Whiff-a-tooty, my gimbo!" Then he would charge off at breakneck speed, not necessarily on his horse. The townsfolk understandably became suspicious.

He had two serious affairs, one with Margaret Chapland, the daughter of Henry Chapland, owner of a racing stables at nearby Berimma Point, and one with her horse, Mabel. It was believed that Margaret was pregnant when the affair dissolved, but as Randolph had by this time run away with her horse, the whole affair was hushed up.

That was the mystery of Coverleigh Estate. What had happened to Randolph? It was as if he had leapt on Margaret's horse one day and ridden off into the sunset, never to be seen again. But that was in 1928, and by this time Eliza and Richard Branwood had already produced a daughter called Augusta. It was Augusta who grew up to inherit Coverleigh Estate, and change the name to Branwood, and she eventually married a fellow called Indigo Appledean, who agreed to change his name on marriage so as to preserve the Branwood name.

Indigo had died at the age of forty in unfortunate circumstances, and it was forbidden to utter his name in the Great Hall while Augusta was around. *She* occasionally mentioned him, though never by name, usually as a passing reference to something else. But it was more than the servants' jobs were worth to voice the name Indigo in Augusta's presence.

Joanne Destry continued to flick through the pages of the family history, scanning each column, looking for the clue that she was in search of. What had happened to Randolph? She had searched every reference she could find in the library at Berimma Point, and after finishing a fine arts degree in the city she had returned to take up a menial position in the household at Branwood.

Loosely, she was Augusta's 'assistant', which could mean anything from tying her bootlaces to driving her into town for medical appointments. It would do for now. Basically, she had more than a personal interest in the fate of Randolph, as her great-grandmother had been a lady called Margaret Chapland.

II

James sat in his office scanning a schedule of fees while the nervous looking gentleman opposite twisted his hat in his hands. George Valentine was fretting dully on his grief, trying to come to terms with his daughter's suicide, and at the same time attempting to tie up the practical side of his daughter's funeral.

'I'm not a wealthy man, Mr. Coverleigh, but I do want the best for my daughter's eternal rest. I need to know how much it will take to secure her a place in 'HEAVEN'.'

'I understand your grief,' Mr. Valentine, 'and I can assure you that we will do the best we possibly can for Elspeth. But there is a bit of a technical problem to be overcome initially.'

James looked at Mr. Valentine with what he termed his 'sublime countenance', which to outsiders meant a sickly smile, somewhat akin to that on the face of a second-hand car dealer when he's telling you that the gearbox has a slight rattle, but is good for 50,000 miles nevertheless.

'You see, as a suicide, Elspeth may not be interred in consecrated ground. In the old days, a suicide couldn't actually be buried in the cemetery at all. They were interred outside the furthermost wall.'

'But that's why I came to you,' said Mr. Valentine. 'She won't be going into the ground, will she? She'll be up in the air somewhere. I took the tour, and I saw the layout.'

'Aah, yes. But you see, under the new regulations as passed by the Second Convention of the International Christian New Wave Post Modernist Aerial Interrologists Association, Article 27, paragraph 16, sub para 3 - and as reiterated in the footnotes at the end of Article 28, it clearly states that the air, consecrated in those sections of Mausoleums exceeding one hundred feet in length and twenty feet in height, before Wednesday August 5th. 2000, and extending to each and any mausoleum of any size erected and consecrated after that date, shall be regarded as 'Heavenly Abodes', and subject to the same restrictions and penalties hitherto and forever encapsulated in our religious rituals as practiced by any Anglican, Catholic, Lutheran, Methodist, Baptist, Presbyterian, New Gospel..... (the list goes on for three pages, Mr. Valentine...) since the first of Henry VIII, after the nobbling of Catherine of Aragon.'

Mr. Valentine shifted in his seat, and irritably destroyed his hat by twisting it in half.

'What the hell has my daughter got to do with Henry VIII and Catherine of Aragon? I just want her to be happy in her afterlife.'

'And she will be, she will be,' James cut in. 'I'm just pointing out the difficulties that I have to circumvent on your behalf. By the way, we prefer the term 'Afterdeath'; it seems more appropriate.'

'Now, let's get down to the nitty gritty. I can see you're a man who doesn't falter once he's made up his mind, so for you, Mr. Valentine, I'm going to put myself out, and work out a once in a lifetime deal.'

George looked bemused.

'Well, it *is* once in a lifetime, isn't it? She's not going to die twice, is she?'

James laughed gently, and rubbed his hands together. 'No, of course not, Mr. Valentine. A slip of the tongue. Now here's where we may help you.' He pulled over a large calculator, and began hitting the keys.

'There'll be the embalming, of course, she must look pretty for your visits in the future, mustn't she? The coffin, we'll come to that later. We have a wide range to choose from of course, but let us say....' and he hit a key. 'Then the Peter's Pence, Purgatory fees, hire of the automatic coffin opener, say three times a day? That will make it less boring for the lass, and automatic promotion in accordance with Article 23 at a monthly rate of.... right! We can fit her in to 'PURGATORY' initially, for an all up $10,200; everything paid for except the automatic promotion. That's another $42 a month for as long as you wish to better her position. Now I can't say fairer than that, can I Mr. Valentine?'

George Valentine sat there in shock. He seemed to find it difficult to speak at first, then said: 'I had no idea it was going to be so expensive! That... that's the best you can do?'

'That's the best I can do if you want to slip your daughter into 'HEAVEN' via the back door so to speak,' said James, raising one concerned eyebrow.

'But I thought you said she could only go to 'PURGATORY',' said Valentine, confused.

'Aah, yes, but as I said, with automatic promotion, the coffins are slowly moved along through the seven levels of 'PURGATORY', and as long as the payments are up to date Elspeth will sooner or later enter those Pearly Gates - via a Pearly side door, actually, being a suicide. But nevertheless, she will get there.'

'What other options are there?' said George, mopping his brow with the remains of his hat.

'We can do a great deal on 'HELL', of course. Then with automatic promotion payments, she could be in 'PURGATORY' within, say, fifty-five years. It's not beyond the bounds of possibility that she could meet up with you in 'HEAVEN' within a hundred and fifty years, Mr. Valentine. That's another option, of course. There's only one downside to that, but it may never happen.'

'What's that?' said George, on the verge of cardiac arrest.

'Well... I hesitate to say! I think you should consider your options without being swayed by the more sordid things which may happen.'

'Well, how much is the 'HELL' option?'

'Let me see...' James clicked away at his calculator, and looked sombre. 'I can offer you a lower level 'HELL' spot, with variable mobility and only temporary damnation for as little as $4,780 and $27 per month.'

'Is the $27 a month on top of the $4,780, or is that to pay it off?'

'Oh, no! No, no, no! The $27 a month is for the variable mobility version of automatic promotion. That means that some months your daughter's coffin will be moved so many spaces and levels in the direction of 'PURGATORY', and some months in the other direction, depending on whether or not she's being overtaken by other coffins. We do guarantee, however, that the overall movement for the year will be a net gain in the direction of 'PURGATORY' - or in other words, she'll get there eventually; probably after about a hundred years. If you should require a sulphur and brimstone filter, there is a small extra charge. But that's up to you. The only disadvantage I can see is that the smell gets into the hair and clothes, so when you come to kiss them it can be rather unpleasant.'

'What was that 'downside' you were talking about before. Was that the brimstone?'

'Oh, no! I was talking about, well... I take it your daughter was a virgin at her departure from this life?'

'Yes. Yes she was, well, as far as I know,' said George.

'Then you probably won't want her interfered with. Some of the visitors to 'HELL' are a little strange. Sometimes, if there is no security around during those times the coffin is open, things can... happen!'

'Do you mean they'd pull her out of her coffin?' said George, outraged.

'No, not necessarily. But she would not necessarily be safe, Mr. Valentine.

'I thought you provided security around the clock,' said George, blusteringly.

'We do, and usually it's okay. But... you know! ... 'HELL'. It's the nature of the place!'

George got up and held out his hand.

'You've been very helpful Mr. Coverleigh. I'll go and see the bank. I think we'll be trying for the 'PURGATORY' option, but it depends on finance. Thank you.'

'...And thank you, Mr. Valentine,' said James as he showed him out.

III

Brindy Somers took the dirt path around the cemetery, and headed for the little church through the trees that she'd heard so much about. She was not much of a one for church, but her imminent demise had changed all that. With less than three months to do something, she felt she needed all the help she could get. Whether that came in the way of a herbal diet, a wonder cure, or a direct line to God didn't really matter.

Pastor Adam Cain opened the door, and looked twice. Brindy was an exquisite looking woman. He couldn't invite her in quickly enough, and he sat her down in his private apartment.

'What exactly can I do for you,' Cain asked, hopefully.

Brindy didn't really know where to begin, and after a few moments just burst into tears.

'Hey, now... don't take on. Let's talk about it,' he said.

'I'm going to die,' she blurted out. 'I'm just going to die, and I can't understand why.'

'What makes you think you're going to die,' he said.

'I have a tumour... on the brain. Not exactly on the brain, but on the cortex, and they say it's inoperable. It's already affecting my vision and my sense of balance, and it gives me these terrible headaches. I haven't got much time.'

'I see! Well, I must say, I'm really sorry to hear it. You look incredibly healthy to me. Just how long do they say you've got?'

'Less than three months, maybe a lot less.'

'You want me to pray for you,' Adam said, uncertainly.

'I want you to save my life! You're a priest, you're supposed to have some clout with him up there. I want you to get rid of this tumour.'

For the first time in his life, Adam was lost for words. He was used to manipulating silly middle aged women, not interceding with God in a real case of life or death. He looked at her flawless beauty, and felt like a fraud. He sat back in his chair and put his hands together, thoughtfully.

'I wouldn't want to give you false hopes,' he began. 'I'm not a miracle worker, and I certainly can't offer you any more hope than the medical profession. For whatever reason - and we must remember that God works in mysterious ways - he has decided that your job here is over, and he needs you elsewhere.'

'Is that the best you can do?' Brindy said, angrily.

Adam looked at her, and suddenly felt like a fool. What was he doing messing about with someone else's philosophy, when he had one of his own? She obviously wasn't going to thank him for being ineffective, or for giving her platitudes.

'No, it's not actually. I could induct you into the Flower of the Flock, but you would have to be cooperative, and I'm not convinced that your state of mind will allow you to cooperate.'

'Try me! What is this Flower of the Flock? What will it do?'

'I'll tell you, but only if you promise to listen without interrupting.'

Adam was not at all sure of himself here. He felt like he was entering a minefield.

'I promise. Just tell me.' Brindy was desperate for good news, any good news.

'The Flower of the Flock consists of a small number of people who are slowly releasing themselves from the urges of the flesh, by a process of over-indulgence. It's our way of preparing for a spiritual re-birth.' Adam waited for the sarcastic response, the cynical laugh, but Brindy just sat and waited.

'Where do I fit in?'

'Well, I happen to believe that the brain is an incredibly powerful organ, capable of curing the body of its ills if only we knew how to use it properly.'

'Yes, go on!'

'I also believe that the strongest impulse we have is the sexual impulse, the urge to procreate.

If we could somehow utilize the power of the brain in conjunction with the drive of the sexual urge, and incorporate these into a spiritual cleansing ritual for the body, we might just be able to cure that tumour of yours. It's a question of focus.'

'You've got my complete attention,' said Brindy. 'Do go on!'

'Well, just imagine a laser beam, aimed at incising that tumour without damaging the surrounding tissue, a beam of light focussed through a ruby with the ability of slicing through tissue with incredible accuracy, and then dissolving the tumour once it has been excised from the cortex. Now imagine a beam of thought, two beams in fact, one from each of us, focussed through the intensity of a mutual orgasm and directed at the incision of that tumour...'

Brindy sat up straight, her mouth fell open.

'Is it possible... do you think it would work? It sounds like it would work!'

'We will never know unless you're willing to try,' said Adam.

'It's the only option I've been given so far, outside of lying down and dying.'

Brindy didn't seem at all shocked by the solution. Sex was not something that she feared, it was merely a physical function. If it would do the trick, then she was prepared to try anything.

'If you're prepared to enter into such a program, I would expect you to sever any ties, certainly sexual ones, with anyone you've been seeing up to now. You would have to follow an exclusive program with me, and me alone.'

Brindy nodded.

'I agree. I'll give it a go. When do we start?'

Adam looked at her thoughtfully. She was a beautiful woman.

'Just give me a day to try and ritualize what we're going to do, so that we can get the greatest impact out of it. It's not going to happen in five minutes, so we'll have to meet on a regular basis, probably every two days.'

'For how long, do you think?'

'For as long as it takes,' he said. Then he showed her out.

Chapter Five

James Coverleigh stomped out of the Great Hall in a foul mood, and headed back to Valhalla where his office was located. He'd just had another argument with Augusta over money, and he was feeling murderous. All he'd wanted was a lousy five thousand to put in a circular fountain outside the entrance to Valhalla, to give it that extra something when visitors arrived. Augusta had laughed at him.

'Goodness boy, when you can learn the value of five thousand dollars, and not squander every penny that God sends, maybe then I might think about it. But you young people today have awfully high expectations for someone without an income of your own. Go and earn the money at Valhalla, and put it in yourself. This family has other priorities.'

It was no good arguing with the old bitch, he thought. You could never win. She held the purse strings, and as long as she did, he would never come into his rightful inheritance.

James was descended along an incidental line, but he was at least a Coverleigh. It was galling to both James and his cousin Agnes that they were true Coverleighs, whereas Augusta was only a Branwood. It infuriated them to play second fiddle to a woman who should never, in their estimation, have inherited the estate in the first place. Unfortunately, the original Sir Jeremy had settled his estates on himself and his heirs male, with contingent remainder to his daughters. This meant that if the direct male line petered out, the estate could be transmitted through the female line. This was what actually happened when Randolph disappeared.

It all went back to Randolph. What had happened to Randolph? There was something very fishy there as far as both James and Agnes were concerned, and although Augusta was not old enough to be involved in his disappearance, her parents were. James had never been able to find any clues to his disappearance, and Augusta refused point blank to discuss it. So there the matter ended. This didn't stop Agnes, however, bemoaning the fact that if she had inherited the estate, things would have been a lot different.

James was more inclined to think that his father, Gordon Coverleigh, should have inherited when the estate passed from Eliza to her daughter on her death in 1971, but it was all conjecture at this stage. The only certainty was that James would inherit when Augusta died. But when? The old bitch was as strong as a Mallee bull. She might be seventy-four, but she could last another twenty years, and James wasn't inclined to wait that long.

He knew that he was anything but a Coverleigh in looks. He was short and olive skinned with black oily hair, and he had a seedy look about him that came from his Spanish grandmother. He looked totally different to his cousin Agnes, who had no Spanish blood at all. Augusta called him the 'little spick' when she was unhappy with him, and she didn't trust him at all. That was probably wise on her behalf, as he disliked her intensely, and kept the peace only because he relied on her financial clout.

Back in the office he turned on the radio, just in time to catch the latest news. The State Parliament had finally passed the country's first Euthanasia Bill. Among its many amendments was the fact that signed permission of the dying member was required, along with two signatures from doctors. The actual euthanasia could then be conducted in any facility registered for that purpose. James smashed his fist into his palm. Yes! At last! He was on to the Department of Health immediately for the forms to register

Valhalla as a lawful venue for conducting a Euthanasia program. They said they'd send them out. As he put down the phone, his cousin Agnes shuffled into his office, and sat down opposite his desk.

'Hello Agnes, what can I do for you?'

James looked at his older cousin through his dark eyes, and hoped that she would make it brief. He didn't have a lot of sympathy for her, as he saw her as a hanger-on who, though an ally, was a pretty ineffectual one.

'I just thought I'd come and see you after Augusta's disgraceful scene today. I overheard what she said about your idea for a fountain, and I thought I'd let you know that I agree with you entirely. I think it's disgraceful the way she controls and manipulates us over money. We should have been given independent means by now, and not be constantly having to go to her cap in hand for anything we need.'

James looked at her with interest. Perhaps she could be useful after all.

'I didn't realize that you were so close when we were arguing.'

Agnes had the grace to blush, and avoid his eyes.

'I just happened to be on my way to the kitchen, and the door was open. I'm surprised that the staff didn't hear her. She was very loud.'

'Isn't she always?' said James, bitterly. 'To be honest Agnes, I'm coming to the end of my rope. I find myself hoping that she'll fall down the stairs and break her neck. She's seventy four, she could keep going for another twenty years, you know.'

Agnes sat up brightly at that. She found the idea of Augusta breaking her neck attractive, if not amusing.

'The way she goes at that horse every morning, she'll probably rupture herself first,' she said, maliciously. James laughed with her, and he motioned her to shut the door. She pushed the door to, and then sat down again.

'Just what are your expectations, Agnes? When I inherit, as I shall one day, what do you get out of it?'

'I shall, of course, rely on your generosity to maintain me in my old age, James. I feel that, besides my keep, I should at least feel independent. Let's say an income of, what, three hundred dollars a week. Also, the use of the car to take me to town when required.'

She sat back and looked at him, her eyes watchful. He twirled a pen on the desk, and a lock of his oily hair fell across his eyes.

'Let's say two hundred a week, and use of the car. All household expenses provided for,' said James, carefully.

Agnes nodded her head, and smiled, brightly. 'I thought I was being a bit hopeful, asking for three hundred.' She laughed, and James gave her a sly smile.

'It's a deal then!' They shook on it.

'Okay Agnes. We have to come up with a plan of action. From now on, anything that's said is between you and me! You talk to nobody, understand?'

'Understood,' said Agnes, her eyes shining.

'Are you aware,' said James, 'that the State Parliament has just pushed through a Euthanasia Bill? All we need is the signature of the intended, and two signatures from independent doctors. I have already applied for Valhalla to be accredited as a place where Euthanasia may be conducted. Do you see where I'm going?'

'I certainly do. If anything should happen to Augusta, anything 'terminal', as long as we had her signature all we'd need would be two tame doctors.'

'You catch on quick. It so happens that I have one 'tame' doctor lined up already, you know who! I have some information about him that would not sit well with the A.M.A. The other doctor, well, we'll have to work on Carstairs somehow. I'll figure that out as we come to it.'

'In the meantime,' said Agnes, 'what is needed is a little 'accident'.'

'I'll leave that in your capable hands,' said James. 'Tell me nothing. It's better that I don't know.'

Agnes left his office with a spring in her step that she hadn't had for years.

II

Eugenia Barry sat and sipped her tea slowly, while Reginald slowly described circles above the floor at the foot of their marriage bed. She wanted to give him half an hour to settle down before calling the doctor. She had been tidying herself up in the bathroom while talking to him loudly through the bathroom door.

'Well, I'm sorry Reginald, but you shouldn't have annoyed me, putting your dirty feet all over my nice kitchen chair. Besides, this hanging fad of yours, it was bound to end badly. I said to myself some months ago that you would make a mistake one day, and that would be it! What would I do then, I thought? I mean, how humiliating to have to admit to the neighbours that your husband has accidentally hanged himself in the bedroom.'

Eugenia brushed her hair, and studied herself in the mirror. There was a nasty spot starting at the edge of her mouth. Oh blast! She hoped it wasn't going to blow up into one of those big yellow pimples. She tut-tutted, and continued brushing.

For a woman of 54 she was still attractive, if only in a cheap sort of way. She had grown up in Port Waterdale behind the Meatworks, in the less savoury side of town. As a young teenager she had discovered that she could get money and sweets if she let the boys put their hands up her dress, and as she quite liked the feeling she saw no objection to gaining by it. The 'town bike' was an epithet applied to her by twenty, and it was only Reginald's docility and stupidity that rescued her from a life on the streets. She still had dark, attractive eyes, though she always overdid the make-up, the lipstick and the eyeliner especially. Conventional wisdom looked at her overdone features, and immediately said, 'Slut'.

'It's a good thing that I've joined the Flower of the Flock, Reginald. I dare say you wouldn't have approved, but there, you never did approve of anything I did. I remember when you caught me with Artie Shorter of the newsagency that time. God, you cut up rough! He was only getting a little comfort, after all, and yet you made a Federal case out of it.'

'That's what I say, Reginald. You never had a sense of proportion. I dare say that you wouldn't have approved of me and the Pastor this morning, either. You're so small-minded. Even if I'd explained about the pastor's desensitising program, I doubt if you'd have understood, *or even tried to understand,*' she shouted around the door, so that he would be sure to hear.

Eugenia walked back into the bedroom and looked up at Reginald's face.

'Oh, for goodness sake! Won't you please put that tongue away. It's disgusting!'

The doctor eventually turned up with the local constable in tow. She ushered them in, wringing her hands together and trying to squeeze out a couple of tears.

'This is so terrible, so awful. I told him a hundred times that he would do himself some damage one day. But he had a spinal problem, you see, and the only relief he could get was by partly hanging himself from a beam, to separate the vertebrae. He must have accidentally kicked the chair over.'

The constable looked up at Reginald, then down at the floor.

'What chair was that, madam? I don't see any chair.'

Eugenia looked, and then realized with horror that she'd forgotten to put the chair back. That's what came from doing things on the spur of the moment.

'Oh, that's right. I put it back in the kitchen. I'm sorry about that, but it's rather a favourite chair of mine, you see, and I saw no sense in leaving it lying on the floor. It was already too late when I found him like this.'

The constable scowled at her, and shook his head.

'Do you realize it's against the law to interfere with a crime scene? Did you try to do anything to save your husband, like picking him up by the legs and taking the pressure off his neck - anything like that?'

'Yes, I did, come to think of it. But I can assure you constable, it was hopeless. He was already dead. I held him up for as long as I could, then I gave in to the inevitable, and I phoned the good doctor here.'

Dr. Carstairs pulled a surgical blade out of his bag, and with the constable supporting Reginald's body slashed through the rope. They then lowered him to the floor, and asked her to stand back.

'Perhaps it would be better if you waited in the other room, Mrs. Barry. We'll attend to your husband.'

She left the room and went and sat in the lounge. The constable looked at Carstairs, and the doctor raised one eyebrow.

'There's a cold fish for you,' said Constable Porter. 'She put the chair back! Whhhooo hooo!!!!'

'I don't think we'll need an autopsy. It's fairly straightforward - he died of a broken neck,' said Carstairs.

'I'll phone for an ambulance to take him to the hospital morgue, and once I've had a more detailed look at him I'll sign the death certificate over there.'

Eugenia's voice rang out from the lounge room:

'So thoughtless of me - would either of you gentlemen care for a cup of tea?'

The two men looked at each other, and in unison, grunted: 'No!'

III

Edmund was a busy boy over the next twenty-four hours. He'd received the plans from Werner von Keppler earlier than he'd expected, and had immediately taken them around to the local engineers, Wally Kirk & Partners. He spent an hour with Wally, going through the plans, and Wally was delighted to get a commission that would tax his brain cells for a change.

'You leave it to me. I'll smooth out the rough edges, and we'll have a working pop-up before you know it,' he said to Edmund.

'How long do you think it'll take?'

'For the first one - a couple of days. I'll just have to get the Perspex sheeting in, the rest of the stuff we'd have lying around here.'

Edmund went off feeling most reassured. The following morning he went in to work to take care of an embalming job that had just come in, poor old Reg Barry, an inoffensive old chap who had accidentally hanged himself the day before.

Edmund had to wash and disinfect the body, shave it, seal the eyelids down with small plastic caps, and tie the mouth shut using small tacks in the upper and lower jaws. He then twisted wire around the tacks to hold the jaw in a closed position.

Noting the broken neck, Edmund made up a fairly sturdy wire frame that fitted tightly around the back of the neck and shoulders, supporting the head. He then prepared the embalming solution, formaldehyde and water mixed in the correct proportions, and placed in a small reservoir attached to an electric pump. Jonathon Pepper came in as he was preparing this, and took a look at the new client.

'Old Reg, eh? I knew she'd do for him one day. She's a hard case that woman. Poor old Reg was a fool to marry her, I told him so at the time. He was too soft for someone like her. She always wanted to wear the pants. She told him she was pregnant, I remember, and he married her. She didn't tell him that the child belonged to Harry Bond. She'd been playing them off against each other.'

Edmund looked up.

'Do you know that for a fact? That must have been forty years ago.'

'Of course I knew it for a fact! Reg and Harry and I went to school together. She was the village bike in those days. I remember trying to warn Reg, but he was a couple of years older than me, he wouldn't listen.'

'Still, I hardly think she'd have anything to do with this. Everyone knew he had a back problem, and that he used to stretch his neck.'

'No-one better than her, eh? I'm telling you, that woman was involved in this. Reg wasn't daft enough to make a mistake like that.'

'Well anyway, pop. We've got him now, and you'll be pleased to hear that I'm going to make him our first pop-up. Wally Kirk reckons that he'll have a working model for us, probably by tomorrow or the day after. I just have to wire his joints so he doesn't fall down and, presto!'

'Well I hope it works,' grunted his father. 'If it does, we'll put on a demonstration for the townsfolk, get them used to the idea.'

Jonathon retired to his office.

Brindy Somers reported in for work just after Edmund had finished hooking up the pump to the carotid artery, and fixing an escape tube to the femoral vein in the groin. As he pumped the embalming fluid in, the blood was forced out of the vein and ran down into the drain. Edmund would flush it later, otherwise there would be a build-up of congealed blood in the drain.

'Hi Brindy. Ready to start work?' Edmund called out.

Brindy nodded, but was strangely subdued. She hadn't spoken to anyone about her tumour to this point except Carstairs, and Pastor Adam Cain. She didn't really want to discuss it with her employers, so she just kept quiet.

'I want you to do a really good job on this one,' Edmund said. 'It's got to last about a hundred years.'

Brindy stopped what she was doing, and looked at him questioningly.

'You don't know it yet, but this fellow is going to go down in history!'

He did a double take on that. To be strictly correct, he was going to 'pop-up' in history. Edmund chuckled to himself.

After suturing the artery and vein, Edmund aspirated the gases and liquids from the abdominal cavity, while Brindy came over to shampoo the hair, what was left of it. She also had to clean the nails and rub cream into the hands and face, to stop dehydration.

She had been worrying over the visit to Pastor Adam's since the day before. Was it the right thing to do? What other course of action was there? Then at home she had begun to think about her relationship with Carstairs, and had a fit of the guilts. It was all so confusing - what she needed was a sign, a sign from God that this program with Adam was the right thing to do. So she began to pray, fervently, that she would be given a sign to instruct her one way or the other. She was busy soaping the hair of the corpse, when Edmund let out an exclamation.

'Well, I'll be damned. I've never seen anything like that before!'

The embalming fluid had done its job well, flowing through the arteries and veins and finding its way into all the capillaries. Too well in fact, because as Edmund watched, Reginald's member began to rise up as if alive, unbent and straightened and shortly became a fully-fledged erection, proudly waving towards the ceiling.

Brindy took a step backwards in shock. Her mouth dropped open, and she said, 'Thank you God! Oh, thank you, thank you!'

Edmund looked worried.

'Are you all right, Brindy?' Surely she'd seen an erection before.

'It's a sign,' said Brindy, 'a sign from God!'

Suddenly she cheered up, and Edmund was surprised to see suddenly the old, happy Brindy Somers emerge in front of his eyes. She really was a very attractive woman when she smiled.

'I don't know about that,' said Edmund, 'but I do know it's going to get in the way. How the hell am I going to get his trousers zipped up with that sticking out like a bean-pole?'

When it came time to dress him, Edmund found that short of amputation there was no way that Reginald was going to fit demurely into his trousers. It would have to remain sticking out, which meant it had to be hidden. Edmund settled on dressing Reginald in an overcoat, and shoving his hands in the pockets, the overcoat would then hang in folds effectively hiding the erection from public view. He had no other choice.

Brindy concentrated on the make-up, and once Edmund had gone she felt safe enough to speak out loud.

'I don't know who you are, mister, but I do know you've been sent from God in answer to a prayer. If that isn't a sign from God, then I don't know what is!'

She lifted the overcoat and peeked at his erection again.

'You're still there, you little beauty,' she said, patting it on the head.

She thought once more about pastor Adam. She'd arranged to see him the next day, after work, and she now knew that it was meant to be. She had a fleeting thought about Richard Carstairs, and shrugged her shoulders. God had given him the thumbs down. She'd call it off tomorrow so that she could soldier on with a clear conscience. She had God's backing now. This was going to work!

Chapter Six

It was getting dark by the time Brindy Somers made her way to the little church amongst the trees. She was not terribly happy, as she'd just had an hour-long scene with Richard Carstairs, breaking off their relationship.

'But what have I done?' he said, miserably. 'You know I love you, Brindy. I will always love you.'

'That's all very well, but it's not going to keep me alive, is it?'

She reached out for his hand and gave it a squeeze. 'This is a matter of life and death for me, Richard. I have to go where someone gives me hope. Pastor Adam has done that, he's going to cure me.'

'You can't believe that,' Richard said, exasperated. 'If that's what he's told you, then he's perpetuating the worst kind of cynical joke on you. Look, I'm a doctor. I didn't just rely on my judgement, either. Your films were seen by the top neurosurgeon in the state. It's hopeless, Brindy. You have to come to terms with that.'

'No, Richard. You're wrong. I tell you, I had a sign from God! A definite sign! It's going to be all right. The tumour is going to be dissolved.'

'How do you work that out,' he said. 'Are you going to pray it gone, or what?'

'Partly,' she said, blushing. 'But we're going to harness the power of the brain through sex, and blast it with twin beams from our orgasms.'

Richard staggered back as if he'd been hit.

'Sex! That dirty little rat! He's having a piece of you, Brindy! He's taking advantage of you. You're an attractive woman with a great body; that's all he can see. He just wants to gratify himself at your expense. You're *my* girl, Brindy, not his. I forbid you to do this!'

'You're beyond forbidding me anything, Richard. It's all off I tell you. I'm a free agent, and I'll do what I like from now on.'

Short of begging her to stay, there was nothing that Richard could do. As he watched her disappearing down the road, he felt a surge of anger rise up in him, and he sat down to think furiously. This wasn't going to happen.

Brindy knocked on the door of the church, and Pastor Adam opened it. He looked nervous, she noticed, which was strange as he usually came over as so self-possessed.

'Well, I'm here,' she smiled, and he beckoned her in. 'Have you worked it all out?'

'Come through,' he said, 'I've been working on a ritual to intensify the effects.'

'I don't understand what you mean by ritual,' she said, taking a seat in his small living area. She looked at the small bed, and an anticipatory shiver ran down her spine.

'The church has always depended on ritual. Everything is ritualistic, from the dress to the ceremonies, to the crucifix, to the chanting, the prayers. All ritual! It's supposed to intensify the religious experience. Well, we're going to use the same devices.'

He knelt on the floor, and bade her to kneel also, facing him. He then said a short prayer.

'Lord, we have come together seeking thy mercy for this young woman, who, without thy intervention, will leave this life before her time is due. We ask you lord, for a miracle, such as you performed during your ministry here on earth. Remove the tumour from her cortex, Oh lord, that she might dwell in peace, and knowing your undying love, for her full three score years and ten. Amen.'

Brindy felt tears spring to her eyes, and whispered 'Amen.'

'Now get undressed,' Adam said, peeling of his shirt. Brindy stripped off quite unselfconsciously, and Adam looked at her magnificent body in awe. She was more than beautiful, she was eternal woman personified. She could have been the original Eve in the Garden of Eden before the fall. They knelt again, facing one another, and he took her in his arms and kissed her.

'Now concentrate on that tumour, feel it at the back of your head, and direct a mental laser beam at it as we make love,' he said, quietly.

She lay on her back and he slipped into her as naturally as opening a book. He moved slowly and gently inside her, and the build-up was quiet and meaningful. She began to be flushed around the cheeks, and he noticed how young she looked, how beautiful, and how desirable. She felt him moving within her, and it was as if a force greater than them both was taking over her body, filling her mind with a white light, teasing her up to the threshold of a climax. When the orgasm came, it took them together, and it was as if Brindy's mind was filled with a white explosion that took away her senses, and left her convulsing in his arms. Adam rolled off her and lay caressing her, his mind blasted by the effort and the concentration.

'God, that was incredible,' he said. Brindy clung onto him, unable to speak.

'I really believe that something happened then,' he said. 'I'm not saying it's a cure, but I think we're on the right track.'

'I had a vision of pure light. I felt it in the back of my head. We've got to do this again,' said Brindy. 'Soon!'

'We will, the day after tomorrow,' said Adam, and they both got dressed.

II

Joanne Destry was taking a break in the kitchen. She had a cup of tea and a doughnut in front of her, and was chatting to the cook, Mrs. Cherry.

'You've been here a long time, haven't you, Mrs. Cherry? You must have seen a few changes in the old place.'

'I certainly have, young lady. Why, I've been here over thirty years, and I've seen them come and go. Of course, it's not like it was in the old days. It was gay and full of people, and there were dinners and parties and always something happening when Mr. Branwood was around.'

'Mr. Branwood? What, the old Mr. Branwood - Richard?'

'No, no, child,' Mrs. Cherry laughed. 'Augusta's husband, Indigo Appledean his name was.'

'Oh, so you remember him!'

'I certainly do. A funny gentleman, not the sort you would imagine with Miss Augusta, but a nice gentleman, nevertheless. He was always very involved with the staff.'

'He died fairly young, didn't he,' said Joanne.

Mrs. Cherry was silent for a moment. She seemed reluctant to talk.

'Well, yes he did, and no he didn't, but it came down to the same thing anyway. I don't suppose they could prove anything now, it's been too long.'

'You have me fascinated, Mrs. Cherry. 'He did but he didn't?' You've got me totally confused. When did he die?'

'It was in 1968. I'd only been here about eighteen months at the time, so I was just the junior in the kitchen, and doing a bit of serving during dinner parties. I knew the master wasn't that well, but he wasn't terminal or anything. He was forty.'

'Yes - so what happened?'

Mrs. Cherry turned and closed the kitchen door.

'Do you know it's more than my job's worth if I talk to anyone about Mr. Indigo.'

She looked at Joanne, intensely.

'Don't worry, Mrs. Cherry. I'm not going to tell anyone.'

'I hope not, young lady. There's only Frederick and I left who remember the events of that day, and we haven't mentioned the matter for years.'

Joanne sat up, fascinated. This was mysterious.

'It was the day of Mark Daventry's funeral. Mark was a family friend, and they decided to hold the service over at the old chapel attached to the funeral parlour – Pepper's parlour that is. They were the only undertakers in those days. There were quite a lot of mourners, and from what I understand, not a lot of space to move. I was back here, preparing the wake of course, so I only heard about it later. Mr. Indigo wandered off somewhere, he was not a well man, used to fall asleep at the drop of a hat. Always falling asleep in fact, the number of times I had to wake him for dinner...'

Mrs.Cherry laughed at the memory.

'Anyway. They had the service, then the mourners wandered over to the graveside, and the pall-bearers went into the parlour to collect the coffin. They walked it over to the graveside and laid it down, the minister went through the ritual, and everyone came back for the wake.'

'In the meantime the coffin was buried, and a temporary marker put in place. It wasn't until a couple of hours later that someone noticed Mr. Indigo was missing. No one had seen him since before the chapel service, but Miss Augusta didn't worry too much because she guessed that he'd gone off to lie down somewhere, the way he often did in the afternoons. But to cut a long story short, he didn't show up. The next day they searched the house from one end to the other, and it's a big house, Miss Joanne. For all the next day Miss Augusta wandered about the house, looking lost. It wasn't until the second day after the funeral that Mr. Benjamin Pepper, the old fellow, Jonathon's father, was going through the parlour, and noticed a coffin that shouldn't have been there. He opened it up, and there was Mr.

Daventry lying there, just as he had been two days before, waiting to be buried.'

Joanne gasped, and put her hand over her mouth.

'Of course, we never did find out for sure. But I overheard Miss Augusta and Dr. Laurens talking about it at the time, and it seems that they thought Indigo had wandered off to lie down, found a nice comfortable coffin and climbed in. Maybe he closed the lid so he wouldn't be discovered, then fell asleep. Anyway, by the time they worked all this out he'd been in the ground for two days. Laurens said they'd better dig him up, but Augusta said no, he'd be dead anyway, and it would cause a scandal. She talked Laurens into signing a fake death certificate for Mr. Indigo, and the next day they held a hurried burial service for the late Mr. Branwood. The coffin they buried that time had Mark Daventry in it.'

'My God!' said Joanne, horrified. 'So they buried him alive. How horrible!'

'Doc Laurens said he could have suffocated before he even went underground. They'll never know, of course, and you just remember, not a word!'

'I won't, I promise,' said Joanne. She just sat there in shock.

III

Indigo Appledean was on someone else's mind that afternoon as well. Augusta was moodily staring out of the window at the cemetery, and her eye passed over the area where Mark Daventry had supposedly been laid to rest all those years ago. She looked indecisive today, unusual for her, but she had felt a shiver pass down her spine that morning as if someone had walked over her grave.

'Wi...lll...iam,' she yelled. 'William! Come out wherever you are. I need you to come with me.'

Dr. Laurens looked sheepishly out of the library, and meekly surrendered himself. He had been off the booze for a day, and never had any courage when he was sober.

'I want you to take me over to the cemetery. I'll use the chair.'

She meant the wheelchair that she allowed herself to be pushed around in when she wasn't feeling well, or needed to feel pampered. Today she needed to feel pampered, and had decided that Laurens was going to be the other half of the arrangement.

'Take me to my husband,' she said.

Wrapping a shawl around her shoulders and collecting a bunch of begonias from the garden, she sat back in the chair and let Laurens push her across the uneven ground. They skirted Valhalla and headed off to the right where both Daventry and Indigo had been lain to rest, just a row apart from each other.

'What do you want to rake up the past for,' growled Laurens, once they were out of earshot of the hall. 'You know it upsets you. I'll have to put up with your hysteria for a week if you go to that grave.'

'I need to go, William. I can't tell you why - maybe it's a premonition. I need to make my peace with Indigo.'

'It's a bit late for that,' said Laurens. 'You should have done that in 1968. There's nothing left to make peace with now.'

'Oh, dear,' said Augusta, suddenly sniffling. 'I know it was very foolish of me, very wrong of me in fact. I should have had him dug up the moment we realized.... but it was already too late by then, you said so yourself.'

'Now hang on, don't put it on to me. You were the one that made that decision, no one else. You didn't want the scandal if I remember rightly.'

'But you agreed at the time,' said Augusta. 'We would have been the laughing stock of the town. We would never have lived it down. You can imagine the jokes that they'd tell the tourists - oh yes, and there's the Great Hall. That's where the fifth incumbent disappeared with his girlfriend's horse, and where they buried the current incumbent's husband alive by mistake. I mean, good God. I would never have been able to show my face in public again.'

'You worry too much about external appearances, Augusta. You always have. If you could just have climbed down to the level of the rest of humanity, perhaps you'd have lived a happier life.'

They were silent as he pushed her between the rows of headstones, until they got to the point where a large black polished headstone rose up on the right. A similar one, but smaller, rose on the left. The smaller one said 'Mark Daventry', and it was by this stone that they stopped. Augusta sat quiet for a while, and then laid the flowers at the foot of the grave.

'I'm sorry, Indigo. If you can hear me, I want you to know that I'm sorry.'

There was a resounding silence.

'I know it was very wrong of me.... but; I mean, who goes off and climbs into a coffin to go to sleep? For God's sake, Indigo, what were you thinking of? How were we to know that they'd picked up the wrong coffin? Until Benjamin Pepper found Mark two days later, we had no idea. That's the honest truth, Indigo, I swear it.'

Augusta went quiet as if waiting for an answer from the depths. There was no answer!

'He's not going to talk to you now,' said Laurens.

Augusta burst out weeping.

'Hang on old girl, there's no need to take on. He's in a better place now, you know.'

'Take me home,' said Augusta, between sobs. 'Take me home, Willy.' Laurens looked at her, almost in sympathy. She hadn't called him Willy for years. He pushed her out of the row, and they turned for home.

'I want him dug up,' she said, after recovering herself. 'I want him dug up, and the coffin opened. I have to know!'

'You have to know what?' said Laurens. 'You can't just go digging him up willy-nilly. You'll need an exhumation order, and for that you'll have to have a reason.'

'What's the good of owning your own cemetery if you can't dig them up?'

'It doesn't work like that, Augusta.'

'What if I want him relocated in Valhalla?'

'Hmmm! Might be a bit difficult. He wasn't embalmed, you know. You couldn't have an open coffin situation. There's probably not that much left of him by now.'

'I don't care. Get onto James, tell him I want Indigo exhumed and prepared for re-interment in 'HEAVEN'. It's the least I can do.'

'He'd have to dig him up at night. You wouldn't want to draw attention to it, or they might just start an investigation. I mean, Dammit! I signed the death certificate!'

'I remember. In that case you'd better cooperate with me, hadn't you! After all, from my point of view it was just an unfortunate accident that I had no control over. With you, it was fraud and collusion to cover up an illegal death. I think they'd roast you at the very least.'

Laurens was silent for a moment, he was puffing a bit by now, pushing her slightly uphill.

'You're a bitch, do you know that, Augusta?'

'Oh, sticks and stones,' she replied, a grim smile on her face.

IV

Agnes spent the next morning skulking in her coffin, looking out over the park from her window as the sun came up. The coffin was her equivalent of a security blanket, and she'd had it raised up at one end so that she could lie in it and still see out of the window of her room. The lining was white satin, and she rubbed this between finger and thumb for comfort, as her other hand was occupied elsewhere. Sooner or later one leg would appear out of the coffin and dangle over the side. That was the point at which she became serious.

Death fascinated her, in all its aspects. She loved dead bodies, and often wandered over to the morgue where the bodies were being prepared for interment. She loved coffins. She liked to be there when the lid was closed, it sent a shiver down her spine of delicious apprehension. She had tried it once, closing the lid of her own coffin as she lay in it, not realizing that this particular model had a snap clasp that locked automatically from the outside. She had spent two hours in absolute terror once she found that she couldn't open it again from the inside, and it was only by her thumping continuously on the side that Frederick was alerted as he came to call her for dinner. Luckily the coffin had a faulty seal, otherwise she'd have suffocated. But it felt like she was suffocating anyway, so she never tried that again. She just watched others being locked in.

Death she saw as a grey lady in a shimmering gown, drifting across the floor to sweep her up into her arms, and carry her off to the netherworld. Here there were lots of large, hairy men with pikes, poking at her and stripping her, and doing all sorts of naughty things to her body. She had, in fact, very little experience of large, hairy men, so she tended to make it up as she went along. Here, in this netherworld region the fires burned cold, and the erections were made of ice.

Once, she had opened her eyes from this daydream to find Frederick busy cleaning the window directly in front of her. His view of her would have been pornographic were he not gentleman enough to confine his gaze to the window itself. He would never think to actually look through it.

Agnes had never married, not because she had anything against the hallowed state, just that no one had ever asked her. She had come close a few times, but had usually managed to misread the signs, and never seemed to know what was expected of her at any specific moment.

Those suitors who expected to try before buying were met with an intractable virgin, whose elevated and untouchable womanhood quickly became less attractive than others' more accessible virtues. Those suitors who required the strictest of old fashioned moral values in their betrothed, Agnes teased unmercifully with an abandonment that shocked them to the core. Consequently they fled in horror, and she sat bemused and abandoned as they disappeared into the arms of her virginal friends.

This did not mean that she was without experience. She'd had a number of flings in her life, but as these had always ended disappointingly she had gradually begun to adopt a number of aches and pains that pointed her in the direction of old age. It gave her something to complain about, and kept further suitors at bay. This did nothing for her unsatisfied desires, but it did save her the humiliation of further rejections.

Now, in her late 50's, all she wanted was security, and freedom from the tyranny of her Cousin Augusta's purse strings. Often, she would sit and watch Augusta from a distance, envying her self-assurance, her arrogance, intolerance, and her wealth. Dislike and humiliation had gradually matured into hatred over the past few years, and Agnes now began to haunt the house looking for opportunities to cause mischief.

The cook became suspicious after catching Agnes going through the cleaning cupboards, checking out the stocks of everything from disinfectant to fly spray. There wasn't much in the way of poisons in the house, certainly nothing that couldn't be identified. Augusta wasn't on any medications that she knew of, despite the presence of her drunken private physician. The woman was too damned healthy by far. So what to do? Agnes went back to the idea of a fall, and looked closely at the stairway. A piece of twine stretched across the stairs early in the morning might do the trick, but it might just trip up Joanne Destry on her way up to wake Augusta.

If she could fix a cord and leave it slack across the stairs until Joanne had gone up, then pull it tight, Augusta was always the first down. In the confusion after Augusta fell, she could remove the cord and no one would be any the wiser. Agnes smiled to herself. She'd do it! She'd set it one night, and do the deed the following morning!

Chapter Seven

James listened to the phone ringing, and almost decided to let it ring out. He'd had a rough day, and just wanted to get home and relax. If this was business... ?

He picked up the phone after fifteen rings. They were persistent, whoever they were.

'James, I need to discuss something with you.' It was Augusta.

'Well, can it wait, Augusta? I'm just about to head off, and I really don't feel like grappling with more problems today. How will tomorrow do?'

'No, James, it must be now. I did ask William to deal with it, but he's obviously very reluctant. I don't think he intends asking you.'

James heaved a sigh, and leant back in his chair, putting his feet up on the desk. A lock of jet black hair fell over one eye, and he shook it away impatiently. He always looked more Spanish when he was annoyed.

'Okay, Augusta, shoot! What's the problem?'

'I want you to dig Indigo up.'

There was a stunned silence.

'What do you mean, Augusta? I can't just go digging people up. Once they're buried, especially after thirty odd years, there's hardly enough of them left to dig up anyway.'

'Nevertheless, I want him dug up. I want the coffin opened, and I want to see him. It's important to me. Just think of it as a whim of an old lady, who isn't long for this world.'

James pulled a face. This wasn't the Augusta he knew.

'I find it hard to believe you're serious, cousin. What's this 'not long for this world' rubbish. You haven't had a day's sickness in your life?'

Augusta stifled a sob. She'd been crying to herself for over half an hour, and it was hard to disguise, even over the phone.

'Is five thousand dollars for a fountain serious enough for you?'

She listened for the reply, but there was just a stunned silence. James dropped his feet off the desk and sat up straight, a grim smile on his face.

'I hear you, I hear you! I suppose blackmail is as good a way as any to get your own way. When do you want it done?'

'Tonight, if possible. I'll get Frederick to help you. I know he won't be good for much, but he can shovel a few spadefuls.'

'Tonight!' James groaned. 'That's out of the question, Augusta. I just haven't got the energy. No, look... I'll do it tomorrow, after dark. If anyone comes along we'll just say we're fixing up a grave that's collapsed. They wouldn't know the difference.'

'Well, if you insist. But I want him moved into Valhalla, into 'HEAVEN', is that understood? I know you must be curious, but I can't tell you why. I just need to see inside that coffin.'

'If you must, you must. But I don't like the idea of putting him in 'HEAVEN', Augusta. He might contaminate the place. He wasn't embalmed, was he?'

'No, we didn't do it in those days. Or should I say, Pepper's didn't do it then. It's funny, everyone does it now.'

'If I put him in 'HEAVEN', the coffin will have to be sealed shut. We'll need a new coffin, too. The one he's in will have rotted.'

'I'll pay for all that. Just let me know the moment he's up on the surface, and I'll come over. I don't care what time of the night you do it, I'll be waiting for you to call me.'

'Okay, but I don't know what all the hurry is about all of a sudden. He's been down there since 1968. Why now?'

'Let's just say I've had a premonition. Maybe I haven't got much longer, and I'd like to tidy up a few loose ends before I move on.'

James was silent for a moment. He hoped Agnes hadn't been blathering in her ear. That could be embarrassing. He pushed his hair out of his face.

'I'll believe it when I see it, cousin. But anyway, tomorrow night, okay. When do I get the five thou'?'

'I'll give you a cheque tonight. Just call in on your way through to the North Wing.'

James had been living exclusively in the North Wing for some time. He tried to avoid the Great Hall as much as possible so he could get a bit of peace. It didn't always work, as Augusta roamed both wings on a regular basis, despite the fact that all her living was done in the central section of the house. But for five thousand dollars - what the hell!

He was no sooner at home that night, than a caller was announced. Dr. Richard Carstairs would appreciate it if he could spare him a few minutes of his time, said Frederick. James groaned again. Was there no peace to be found that day?

'Show him in,' he told Frederick, who shortly ushered a dishevelled looking doctor into the room. He looked like he'd been pulled backwards through a hedge.

'God, Richard, you look like crap,' James exclaimed. 'What the hell have you been doing?' Richard slumped into a chair looking totally miserable.

'She's dumped me,' he said, in explanation. 'Brindy's dumped me!'

James looked bemused; he had no idea that there was anything on the boil between the doctor and his part-time make-up artist.

'Brindy Somers you mean? Have you been seeing her?'

'I thought you knew. I thought everyone knew. I wanted to marry her, but everything's fallen apart in the past week.'

'I'm sorry to hear it. But that doesn't explain why you look like that, nor what you want with me if it comes to that.'

'I know, I know! I owe you an explanation. The fact is – Brindy's dying!'

James sat up at that. He looked shocked.

'Are you pulling my leg?'

'No - brain tumour. Actually a tumour on the cortex; you know what that is. It's inoperable, anyway. She was having vision problems and headaches, and now I understand she's having balance problems. It's all symptomatic. We did all the usual tests, and the x-rays showed up a large mass on the cortex. I got a second opinion from Sir David Jordan, and he agrees. Totally inoperable, just a question of time.'

'How much time has she got - or don't you know?'

James was thinking more of having to replace his make-up artist than how unfortunate his employee was.

'Three months or less. Could be a lot less. If it's a really aggressive tumour, she could be dead in a week.'

'I don't get it, then. Is she just trying to protect you, or what? Why would she dump you now?'

Richard shook his head, miserably.

'That new preacher, the hippie type who's camping out in the old Wesleyan Church. He's convinced her that he can cure her - by having sex with her.'

James suppressed a smile. He knew he shouldn't rub it in, but he was amused.

'She believes that, does she? I didn't think she was the gullible type.'

'Neither did I. But she's gone off, and tonight she was with him - and it's driving me crazy. I followed her. I got down in the grass and crawled along on my hands and knees, me, a respectable doctor for god's sake.'

James looked enlightened. No wonder he was such a mess.

'I went around the side of the church where he'd made a sort of chimney, and I could hear everything. He told her to strip off, and she did, without a murmur. Then he had sex with her. I tell you, I'm going quite mad at the thought of it.'

James shook his head, as if in sympathy. In fact he was thinking, 'how long is this going to take? I just want to relax, for god's sake.'

'I can appreciate your position...' said James.

'But you don't know why I came to talk to you about it. No, you wouldn't, I haven't been very specific have I? Well I'll tell you; I want her body.'

James eyebrows shot up half an inch. Then he sat back, and his eyes narrowed in thought. He looked a bit like a cunning gypsy at such moments, his olive skin accentuating his features.

'I want her body when she's dead, that's what I meant to say. I may not have her while she's alive, but with your help I could have her when she's dead.'

'Now hang on a minute,' said James. 'I don't know whether I want to hear any of this.'

'I thought you might say that. But you're the only one I can turn to. She and I have been as good as married for months. This thing with the preacher, it's just an aberration. She's clinging to a forlorn hope that she's going to get better. In actual fact, she'll get a lot worse, may even go stark staring mad before the end. Or she might just become paralysed. Whichever way it goes, her body will suffer. She has the most beautiful body I've ever seen, and she stands a chance of ruining it by allowing this thing to run its course. I want her body as it is now, embalmed, and laid out in my cellar forever, so I can see her whenever I want. It sounds crazy I know, but she's going to die anyway. What's a few weeks? I want you to help me embalm her.'

James looked at him in silence, then bit the inside of his cheek, a sign that he was thinking furiously.

'What do I get out of it,' he said. 'It's a hell of a risk! What's in it for me?'

'Name your price. What would you want?'

'I'm thinking more of goods in kind. Valhalla is in line to become a licensed Euthanasia Facility in the near future. I may need to bend a few rules from time to time.'

'I see; and I'm a doctor. Okay, you could say that my signature might be available under certain conditions. You scratch my back....'

James nodded to himself. This could be the leverage he'd been hoping for.

'An interesting proposition! But what happens if you get sprung with the cadaver at some time in the future. Where will you say you got it from?'

'I'll say I used the hospital morgue to embalm her. You won't be implicated at all.'

'You'd better let me know when you'll want to use our facility, Doctor. It will be a night job I should imagine. Not in the next few days, okay? I have too much on at the moment.'

'Next week then!'

'Next week it is.'

II

Joanne Destry took advantage of the fact that Augusta was 'off-colour' to shoot off to the South wing once again. She hadn't explored it all, not by any means; and she intended to search the building room by room until she discovered some clue as to the fate of Randolph. She was convinced that such a clue existed, but would she recognize it even if she found it?

She bypassed the library this time, and made her way along the passages that led to the old ballroom, the study, and some guest-rooms on the ground floor. The ballroom was a noble ruin; the decorations from some long ago Christmas function were still partly in place, and partly trailing across the old wooden floor. Everything was thick with dust, and it would not have surprised Joanne to see ghostly figures weaving across the floor in a timeless dance. Doors and passageways led off this area, and Joanne could see that she would get lost if she wasn't very careful.

There was still a considerable amount of furniture in the South wing, most of which was antique, and which a collector would die for. But a lot had been moved, witness patches of carpet that were brighter in their colours than the rest, where heavy objects had obviously sat for many years before disappearing and leaving empty spaces. The rooms themselves were less than interesting. Most of the smaller rooms had been used for guests staying over the weekend, and there was nothing really to look at.

Joanne went from room to room, disappointed in her search, until she came to a small room tucked away behind the ballroom, and set into a large alcove. The door was stiff and swollen in its frame. It took a considerable amount of heaving to get it to move at all, and when it did, it creaked.

Once inside, it looked more like a large cupboard than a small room. A desk was built-in against the opposite wall, and there were a number of pigeon holes ranged up the wall. Most of these were empty, but some contained documents and letters thrust in apparently haphazardly. There were also maps and plans, rolled up and stored in shelves on the left, and Joanne stood in the doorway, her heart in her mouth. Shutting the door behind her, she turned on the light and sat at the desk. A quick perusal of some of the documents showed that they were invoices and receipts from the 1940's to the

1960's, many of them concerned with catering, obviously for large parties and gatherings. There were statements for building work on the South wing, and specific work on the ballroom including the installation of a crystal chandelier.

Joanne moved to the maps and plans. Most of these were much older in their origin, some so dry and brittle that unless you were careful, they broke apart. She saw dates of 1914, 1892, 1886, and the oldest, most brittle, was dated 1861. This was an architectural drawing of the Great Hall, without either the North or South Wings. There were features that had obviously never been incorporated into the original building, square towers at each side of the main hall. There was also a portico, supported by six fluted columns in the original drawings, and if this had ever been built, it was certainly not there now. The date of 1861 made it obvious that this was the original plan, as the first part of the building wasn't completed until the end of the following year.

The next plan she looked at was an overall map of the estate, the entire thousand acres. The eastern boundary disappeared into a pine forest, and incorporated a small lake. There was a little holiday shack there these days, but that had only been erected in the 1940's. There was no sign of any other building on the map except the Great Hall itself. On the western side of this was an early indication that the cemetery was already in use, as there were a number of plots identified by numbers, 32 in all. Joanne looked for a date on the map, but there was nothing on the front to identify it. As she rolled it up again, she noticed that someone had scribbled on it, in ink that had turned brown, 1881.

Just as she put it back on the shelf, she stopped and listened. She could hear footsteps in the distance, coming from the direction of the ballroom. It was a steady, measured tread, nothing rushed about it. She got up and stood behind the door, pulling a face at her predicament. Her presence in the South wing wasn't a capital offence, but she didn't really have a covering story prepared. She listened as the footsteps continued along the far passageway, and somewhere in the distance a door opened and closed. Then there was silence.

Releasing her breath in a sigh of relief, she sat down again, and waited. How was she going to get out again without being seen? She decided that she'd wait half an hour, then, if there were no further footsteps, she'd get out in a hurry. The distraction had put her off, and she didn't open any further documents. Half an hour later, she left quietly, pulling the door shut behind her.

III

George and Amelia Valentine sat in the front row of the little chapel, handkerchiefs in their hands. Seven relatives and friends made up the rest of the congregation, a sad tribute to Elspeth's youth.

Elspeth lay in the coffin with the lid open, looking innocent, pure, and beautiful in death. Mrs. Valentine suppressed a sniffle, as the two Valkyrie maidens walked slowly along the aisle. Following them were the pall bearers, a slow march in black suits. In Viking mythology the Valkyrie were the maidens known as *'the choosers of the slain'*. James had done his homework on this, and decided that a couple of good-looking Valkyrie would lift the service a bit, and fit in with the overall concept of Valhalla. So he got a couple of local blonde girls to plait their hair, wear Scandinavian dress, and don imitation Viking helmets he'd had knocked up by Wally Kirk.

All they had to do was advance up the aisle, continue on to the coffin and take up a stance opposite, pointing to the corpse. After holding this pose for ten seconds, they stood aside to allow the pallbearers to close the coffin lid, and hoist Elspeth up on their shoulders. The Valkyrie then led the procession out of the chapel and over to the columned entrance to Valhalla. Outside the huge oak doors one of the Valkyrie took a hunting horn from beside one of the pillars, and blew one long, piercing blast. The doors slowly swung open, and the party continued inside to 'PURGATORY'. The coffin was laid in front of a huge metronome, which ticked away inexorably, reminding everyone that time stops for no man.

Then James stepped forward.

'All of us are gathered here to celebrate the life and the passing of Elspeth Valentine, born 27th January 1983, passed into the Afterdeath, 16th June, 2001.'

James wore a white surplice over his coat, giving him the air, if not the authority, of a man of religion. His dark features made him look a little Greek Orthodox, and he looked at the sparse congregation and continued.

'Elspeth showed great promise as a child, exhibiting a precocious ability in art, especially in the medium of crayons. Her later watercolours bear testimony to this early promise, and her parents treasure her 'Barby Doll Melting on Barbecue', and 'Long Green Stripes on Yucky Grey Background,' both completed, extraordinarily, before the age of six. At nine Elspeth was showing an early interest in the medical profession, and there still exists a photograph of her in white nurse's uniform with a large red cross on the front, attending to a wart on her grandfather's nose while he was asleep. If not the medical profession, she would probably have made a more than competent Vet, as her ministrations to the dog and two cats in the family were consistent with her interest in the orifices of mammals.'

James stopped and cleared his throat.

'It is probably true to say that Elspeth was one of those extraordinary people who would have been capable of following any number of professions, as the innate talent was there, waiting, like plasticene, to be formed and shaped. She made an early decision to quit school, at the age of fifteen, when the world of commerce beckoned. She realized that first-hand experience would be invaluable in her later professional life, and took an interim position in Mrs. O'Leary's Delicatessen, being placed in charge of the cut meats section within only the first three months. During this period she put her spare time to good use, developing an interest in hairdressing, and she could often be seen evenings, assisting Mrs. Trott in the preparation of her home clients. Mrs. Trott assures us that Elspeth had the soft touch necessary for advancement in the trade, and it was only the unfortunate application of a certain type of peroxide to Mrs. Chapman's hair which made her take stock of her future, and develop her interests in another direction.'

Mrs. Valentine let out a little 'whoop' at this, and sobbed into her handkerchief.

'Elspeth then began to cultivate a growing interest in pharmaceuticals, and in her mother's medicine cupboard she discovered any number of medications with which she could gain practical knowledge. She taught herself the finer art of mixing and matching, inventing in the process some of the more exotic designer drugs that are so popular amongst young people today. Some of her concoctions, indeed, were unknown to medical science until she was delivered, unconscious, to the local hospital, suffering from a terminal dosage of a large number of medicants. Thus the short but event-filled life of Elspeth Valentine came to an end, but who can say it was wasted? What this young girl's life tells us is that nothing is ever achieved without sacrifice, and Elspeth was prepared to face up to that sacrifice by trying her own medications, before allowing them to be released on the general market for public use. We say then, farewell Elspeth Valentine, though not goodbye. For Elspeth will continue in this earthly toil, working her way through the maze of 'PURGATORY', ascending through trial and tribulation to the seventh level, before being marched through those pearly gates to the triumphant sound of Gabriel's Harp. It is here then that we leave you, Elspeth, to accustom yourself to your new element, and in the hope that your mother and father may, one day, be re-united with you in the highest realm of the gods. Amen.'

The mourners slowly began to clap, and James smiled and made a half bow. Mrs. Valentine hung onto her husband's arm and smiled up at him.

'That was lovely, wasn't it George?' she said. He stared at her, but made no comment. It was a funny sort of Protestant service to his mind. What was all that about 'the realm of the gods?'

James put his arms in the air to attract everyone's attention.

'Just before you go, ladies and gentlemen, Mrs. Valentine would like to invite you over to her place for a spot of tea and some delicious lamingtons - I believe she made them especially for the occasion. A hand for Mrs. Valentine everyone.'

They all clapped politely,

The doors swung shut behind them as the funeral party walked out into the night, and George walked over to hand James a bank cheque for $10,200. Elspeth's coffin was thrown onto a conveyor which whisked her up to level 3, row 6, coffin 23. A label printed with her name on was affixed to the side of the coffin, and the lights went down for the night.

Chapter Eight

It was just getting dusk when Edmund and Werner von Keppler made their way to the gravesite of Reginald Barry. The workmen had done their part, the hole had been dug vertically nine feet deep, and a square shaped steel sleeve had been inserted to stop the sides from falling in. Lying beside the grave were the parts necessary for construction of the 'pop-up', and it was Werner's job to assemble it.

The design was simplicity itself. A steel rail with corrugated teeth was held by steel C-channel, implanted in the ground and set in concrete at the bottom. This was at the back of the proposed pop-up. The rail was to be affixed to the rear of the Perspex upright coffin; a car starter motor mounted just below the surface would then drive the rail up or down, taking the coffin with it. For this prototype there were terminals at the gravesite ready to plug a car battery into, and a small pedestal beside the grave held an ignition lock, activated by a key.

'Now for zuh big test. I t'ink ve haf no problems, ya!'

'I hope not, but like everything, we can always adjust the design later,' said Edmund. 'I just want to make sure that the motor is strong enough to drive the coffin up or down easily, under full load.'

Keppler snorted.

'Zis motor vill drive anyt'ink. High torque. It usually drives zuh flywheel in zuh car, and zees are not light.' He bolted the perspex and the rail together, and stood it up. They had deliberately chosen this time of day so they wouldn't be observed. They didn't want Valhalla getting onto the idea too quickly in case Jimmy Coverleigh stole their thunder.

Edmund helped Werner stand the coffin up and slide it into place. Rails on the front corners kept it square in the hole, and between them they wiggled it down a foot where it became more stable.

'Zis front comes off to put zuh body in place, zen slides back on, airtight. Try zuh motor now, here is zuh key.'

Edmund fitted the key into the lock while Werner hooked up the battery.

'Later you vill haf zuh 12 volt power line running beside zuh graves, so zey vill be active all zuh time. Zen zuh people vill be able to pop zem up all in zuh line. Zis is revolutionary idea! I t'ink it vill catch on kvik.'

Edmund twisted the key, and the coffin shot down into the hole at about thirty miles an hour, stopping with a loud thump.

'Whoa - I think we'll have to gear that down a bit. I want a nice slow delivery, something with a bit of dignity. I'll bring it back up.'

He twisted the key again, and the coffin rushed up out of the ground like an express train, shot two feet in the air, and toppled over.

Werner laughed.

'I t'ink someone haf heart attack if body shoots up like zat. I vill slow it down. Ve may need t'ree phase power to get sufficient torque. Zair again, zuh coffin's empty. Once zuh body's in it, it vill slow down. But I must put a stop on zuh top so zuh motor cuts out before shooting it out of zuh hole.'

'It will also have a cap on the top, holding the headstone, and that will add a bit of weight. Well, it looks good so far, just a couple of minor adjustments to make.'

It was well and truly dark by this time, and the cemetery had become quite eerie. There was a light mist at ground level, flowing over the graves, and the headstones stood up out of it like sentinels.

Over the other side, by the light of a small torch, James and Frederick were toiling away at Indigo's grave, digging out the first few feet of soil. The headstone proclaiming it to be Mark Daventry had been pulled out and shunted aside, and they took it in turns down in the hole. Frederick had not been too happy about the situation, but like the good servant he was, bent his back to the task.

'I don't know why Augusta has suddenly decided to dig him up,' James grumbled. 'She's had thirty three years to think about it, why now?'

Frederick knew better than to try and answer that. His place was to dig, not provide philosophical conversation. Besides, Frederick knew only too well why Augusta wanted to dig him up, whereas James had no idea. It had all happened before James was born, and no one ever talked about it. Augusta felt that the less who knew, the better.

Frederick was up to his chest by now; just his head and shoulders showing. James stood looking down into the grave as the hole began to fill up with mist.

'It's a bit spooky, isn't it,' said James. 'This bloody mist! They say that there was a mist like this the day Randolph disappeared.'

'They do indeed, sir. He galloped off into the night like the headless horseman, and for nights afterwards you could hear the hoof-beats echoing under the ballroom. My father was the butler in those days, and he used to tell it to us like a ghost story.'

Suddenly there was a piercing shriek, which came from the other side of Daventry's grave. James almost jumped out of his skin, while Frederick's eyes rolled up into his head, and he fell flat on his back in the hole. A figure rose up slowly out of the mist, partly obscured by the headstone.

'Hello chaps! I wondered what was going on over here, so I thought I'd take a look,' Edmund grinned, as James staggered over to sit on a grave.

'You fucking bastard, Pepper! You nearly gave me a bloody heart attack. Look at Frederick - I think you've done for him!'

'Just a little atmosphere, fellas. What's a cemetery without a disembodied soul or two? That was a pretty good shriek, wasn't it?'

'Well you'd better get down that hole and revive poor old Frederick. He's seventy-three, you know. Something like that could kill the poor old bugger.'

'Don't take on,' said Edmund, still grinning, as he jumped down into the hole. He slapped Frederick gently about the face until he showed signs of recovery, then climbed out again.

'So who are you digging up - Mark Daventry?' he said, reading off the headstone. 'Who the hell was he?'

'A friend of the family, years ago. Augusta has decided to put him into Valhalla at her own expense.'

'So you got an exhumation order,' said Edmund, slyly.

'Now see here, Edmund. Don't go stirring up things you don't know anything about. This is just a family thing, understand? We don't want any trouble.'

'Oh, no trouble, James. But I think you owe me one, all right?'

'Okay,' said James, heavily. 'Now hows about you pissing off and letting us get on with it.'

'No probs, James my lad. I'll see you around.' Edmund skipped off between the graves and was soon hidden by the mist.

Frederick dragged himself shaking out of the hole, and sat down on a headstone.

'Excuse me sir, but I thought old Randolph had suddenly turned up again. He was quite mad, you know. He used to roam abroad at night howling at the moon, and they say buggerising horses and cattle. It was his father who used to get into the sheep.'

'It's all right, Frederick. Edmund ought to know better than to go around scaring people at night in this place. He could have done for us both. Well, so much for secrecy. It's out of the bag now. Let's get this finished!'

James jumped into the hole and attacked the remaining earth with vigour. He struck the coffin within a minute, and then just had to clear a way around it. Shortly he managed to lever up one end, and between the two of them they pulled it out of the hole.

James had a trolley with him, so they loaded the coffin onto that, and pulled it out of the way, while they filled the hole in, replacing the headstone where it was.

'I'll have to get some earth to top that up,' said James. 'It's a bit low now.'

They pulled the cart over to the safety of Valhalla, and secreted it inside. Then James phoned Augusta.

'You can go back now, Frederick. Thank you for your help.' Frederick left.

Augusta appeared twenty minutes later, rugged up in an overcoat against the chill, and minus the usually ever-present Dr. Laurens.

'I told William to stay. I wanted to do this on my own. Do you think it will be very dreadful?' said Augusta, looking at the battered coffin.

'It's what you wanted,' said James, unfeelingly. He wasn't in the mood to be sympathetic.

'Shall I open it now?'

'Yes,' said Augusta, shivering, and half turning away.

James pried open the coffin lid, and swung it upwards. They both then stood back with their mouths open. Apart from fifteen bricks, the coffin was empty. Augusta approached it in disbelief. She ran her hand over the inside, and there, alongside the lining, was a letter. She held it up, and then handed it to James, indicating that she wanted him to read it. She couldn't speak.

James opened the single page and read:

"Augusta,

Sorry to take off like this, but after fifteen years of marriage to you, I feel like I've already disappeared. To all intents and purposes I ceased to exist once I allowed myself to lose my independent income, and became beholden to you for everything god sent. You took my name away when we married, and everything else since. I wish you the best for the future, as I wish for myself. You may not have noticed, but Anne Harringay and I have been somewhat close over the past few months, and we have decided to elope.

She's had enough of that nit of a husband, and I've had enough, full stop. I'm not silly enough to expect any pecuniary help from you, so I won't ask. We will probably leave the country.

Just one word of advice - be happy. Climb off your high horse and get down and muddy your hands a little. You will enjoy life a lot more.

Indigo Appledean"

PS - you'll only get this if you have me dug up, and I'm not sure that I'm important enough in your eyes to overcome your natural objections to a scandal.

Augusta listened to James read it, then let out a long wail and toppled to the ground, sobbing.

'Indigo - you left me! How could you do that?'

II

Pastor Adam Cain had been mooning about like a lovesick girl for the previous two days. A vast change had come over him since Brindy's visit, and he realized that whatever came of this relationship, his world was about to change forever. He didn't go out at all, but sat staring into his fire and thinking of this miraculous woman who had come into his life just as she was about to depart her own.

Adam had always prided himself on being untouchable where it came to women. It was very nice being able to command sexual obedience from numbers of women, and treating them like an extended harem. It was nice also that following the sex, the tithes came thick and fast, and his bank account was showing a healthy balance of some thousands. But he hadn't counted on becoming emotionally involved with any of them, and yet this he finally had done. He was in love.

On top of that, however, the sex they'd shared had blown his mind inside out, and left what he thought was a lingering piece of goodness in his heart, a feeling that he'd never had before. He'd always been a straightforward physical animal up until now. A good orgasm was usually enough. Love was for everyone else; he'd just take the sex. Once he'd saturated an area, he'd move on and form his flock elsewhere.

Eugenia Barry, his newest convert was proving to be a bit of an embarrassment where it came to sex. The woman may have been fifty four, but she was insatiable, and used any and every excuse to call by each day for further instruction in deviation.

'I just thought I'd call by, Pastor, because I've had this intense erotic sensation that I've never felt before. I thought I'd ask you about it, because you're so good with these things.'

'Just where is this sensation, Eugenia? I'm not sure that I can help in every instance.'

Adam was desperately trying to think of a way of putting her off, but she was equally determined to be satisfied. With Brindy now on the horizon he didn't really want to continue.

'I think that I'm going to ask Brother Henry to take you in hand,' said Adam. 'He will attend to you with care, and will gradually desensitize you as our program requires.'

'But I want you to do it,' said Eugenia, desperately. 'You've been so good to me, I feel that I owe you so much.'

'Yes. But I have a large flock, Eugenia, and that's the way it works. The pastor can't attend to everyone individually.'

Eugenia finally gave in, and was leaving just as Brindy approached the door. She glared at her in undisguised malevolence, and trotted off back through the trees, muttering to herself.

The ritual was completed again, the same as the first time, only this time the familiarity of it seemed to intensify the experience. Brindy went into convulsions again as she climaxed, and didn't stop for over five minutes. Her mind was filled with a brilliant white light that incorporated a pale blue flame, burning and slicing at the tumour in her brain. Adam lay mentally exhausted.

'I think I love you,' he muttered, almost to himself, as he lay totally sated.

Brindy stirred next to him, and sat up.

'What did you say?' she said, surprised. 'Did you say you loved me?'

'I... er... yes, I think I....'

'Don't ever say that again,' she snapped. 'I'm here for one thing, and one thing only, to get rid of this tumour. You don't honestly think I'd be here if it wasn't for that, do you?'

Adam gasped at her cruelty. He was lost for words.

'We have an agreement, it's to cure me. Don't let it get personal,' she said, pulling her clothes on. 'I'll be back in two days.'

Pausing at the door she looked back at him, hesitating.

'I'm sorry, but you're just not my type, not my type at all,' she said.

When she'd gone, Adam felt his eyes well up with tears.

Richard Carstairs came bounding out of the bushes as Brindy headed back through the trees. He looked like someone demented, his hair awry, his clothes filthy.

'So that's where you've been, you slut,' he growled as he caught up with her. 'Selling yourself cheap to that phoney preacher.'

'Leave it off, Richard,' Brindy exclaimed. 'I told you before, we're finished!'

'No we're not, not by a long shot,' Richard replied, grabbing her arm.

'If you don't let go of me I'll call the police,' she snapped.

'What's got into you, Brindy? Everything was so good, and now you're acting like some common slut.'

'I'm doing what I have to do. It's not your life that's at risk here.'

'I can't let you do this,' Richard said, desperately. 'He's just got you sucked in. He can't cure you any more than I can.'

Brindy turned to look at him with a cold, appraising stare.

'Oh, no? Well I think he already has. My headaches are gone. And my vision has righted itself.'

'That's just a short term thing, Brindy. It won't last. The next stage is madness. You're going to go mad!'

'You're well rid of me then, aren't you? Who wants to go out with a mad woman?'

'I told you I'd stand by you until the end,' Richard said, aghast.

'That's the trouble, Richard. It's all negative negative negative with you. You don't want me to survive. You want me dead. It would be easier. Then you could go through life telling everyone about this woman you almost married, how wonderful she was. You could hold anniversaries every year and cry into your beer. You expect me to be happy having no hope at all.'

'Do you want me to lie to you?'

'No, I want the truth. Adam's giving me the truth; he's curing me. Well, maybe it's not him; maybe he's just the vehicle for a higher power. But I know this, whatever it's doing, it's powerful, and it's good; and I feel better for it.'

She shook him off and headed homewards. Richard threw his hands in the air and sat down, his back against a tree.

III

The following morning there was a new corpse for Edmund to lay out. He pulled the sheet back and saw that it was Mrs. Bacon, his old primary school music teacher. As a small boy he'd had quite a crush on Mrs. Bacon. She'd been in her early thirties then, and was a good-looking woman. He had stalked her around the school, looking love-lost, until another teacher had grabbed him and warned him off. It was a bit hard on a nine-year old.

Now here she lay, at his mercy at last. He pulled back the sheet and took great satisfaction in exposing her entire body. Even at fifty-nine, and dead, she wasn't unattractive. He noted the colour of her pubic hair - 'I always knew she was a bottle blonde', he thought to himself.

Around lunchtime, Jonathon came in with Werner in tow. They'd been having a discussion about computerisation and robotics. Werner had been telling Jonathon that there was nothing that couldn't be done these days with robotics, even when it came to cadavers. Jonathon was extremely interested, as he was still looking for ways to beat Valhalla at their own game.

'I think we might have another goer,' Jonathon said to Edmund. 'How about 'Sentinels', guards for the family vaults? There's more and more vandalism around cemeteries these days, and a lot of vaults have been broken into and vandalised. If we had a coffin each side of the entrance, inside, which would fly open on the entry of intruders, with the corpses sitting up and laying about them with nightsticks, I don't think the intruders would hang about for too long, do you?'

Edmund looked somewhat cynical.

'Why not just give them sub-machine guns. Then they could blast anyone that came in through the door.'

'Zat is a great idea. I like it! Ve could get zuh doors to shut first, zen blast zem to bits. Who would look for zem in a cemetery vault?'

Jonathon hurriedly pooh-poohed the idea.

'Take no notice of Edmund, Werner. That's just his idea of a joke. I think we'd better keep within the law.'

'It zuh pity.' said Werner, his anarchistic mind ticking over. 'Ve could get rid of a lot of scumbags.'

'Anyway, whose corpses are you going to use for these 'Sentinels'? I don't think people would like having their loved ones recruited to look after the rich.'

'We'd just use down-and-outs. They can't afford funerals anyway,' said Jonathon. 'That way they'd get a free berth in a family vault. Quite cozy from their point of view.'

Jonathon saw the new arrival under the sheet.

'Who's the new client? Anyone we know?'

'My old music teacher, Mrs. Bacon,' said Edmund.

'There's one for you, Werner. You can have a practice on her, show us what you can do,' said his father.

Edmund looked mystified, but three days later he was to find out.

Chapter Nine

Agnes had been lying low for a couple of days, worrying about the approaching 'accident'. What if she didn't manage to pull it off? What if she was caught? She would be turned out of the house with no support at all. At her age she couldn't support herself. Maybe she should just wait until Augusta died, that would be the safest course. After all, could she trust James?

He might just be egging her on for his own purposes, with no intention of sticking to his side of the bargain. What could she say, after all? She couldn't blackmail him into keeping their deal, as he would just deny it, and she would end up out in the cold, anyway. These thoughts and others spun around in her head, making her feel quite dizzy at times.

She hadn't seen Augusta because on the previous day Augusta had taken to her bed for no apparent reason, and refused to come down. Even Joanne didn't know what was wrong with her. It seems that she just lay there, alternately weeping and staring at the ceiling, and she wouldn't eat a thing. That afternoon Agnes went for a walk, and found Dr.

Laurens skulking behind the North Wing, a bottle of Jim Beam in his hand.

'Aah, Agnesh my dear. Come to join me in a drinksh?'

'No, William, I have not. Why aren't you with Augusta? I hear she's really upset, crying and carrying on - though what over I have no idea.' Agnes perched herself on the edge of a bench.

'Oh, Augushta, pushta. She's jus' being Augushta! She's a maniac, d'ya know that, Agnesh. She's drunk with power.'

'You're a great one to talk about being drunk. Really!'

'What, me? I'll be sober tomorrow, she'll shtill be drunk with power! Power over you, power over me! Where dush it all end, Agnesh, I ask you. Where dush it all end?'

'I find this a very strange commentary, coming from you, William. You've been with Augusta for years. If that's the way you feel, why stay?'

'I'm jush waiting for her to… die!' said William, blurting the word out. 'Once she diesh, I'll pish off!'

'William! Really! That's a terrible thing to say.'

'She'sh a terrible womans, Agnesh. She'sh downright dangeroush! She doesn't care about anyone elsh, only her.'

Laurens sat back on the bench and nodded to himself, as if what he was saying made perfect sense. Agnes looked at him, and wondered.

'I don't suppose there's any chance of that in the near future, William. Though you should know. You're her doctor after all.'

'There'sh every chansh, if I can get my handsh on her on a dark night. Every chansh in the world. She knows things, Agnesh, she knowsh things that could put me in jail, 'n I'm not goin' to jail for her or anyone.'

Agnes perked up at this.

'I seeee! So William, what are you going to do about it?'

Laurens was silent for a minute, and then he turned to her and grinned.

'I'm going to get *you* to poishon her! Hah!' Then he laughed, a deep bellowing laugh, while Agnes made frantic signs for him to shut up.

'That's a dreadful thing to say, especially for a doctor. What makes you think I want to poison her?' Agnes looked fearful.

'Cosh you do! I know,' he said, touching the side of his nose. 'I've known for a long time. An' you're not the only one. So does Jamesh! Can you blame him? If you don' poishon her, she might go on forever - *forever!*'

'I'd be arrested,' said Agnes, plaintively. 'I'd end up in jail for the rest of my life.'

'No, you wouldn't. What d'ya think I'm a doctor for? I'd sign the death shertificate, natural deash. Old age! She's 74 ya know. Lotsa people die before 74.'

'Would you - really?' said Agnes, hope forming in her breast.

'Of coursh I would. Only too happy.' He looked at her and grinned a lop-sided grin. 'You can bet on it!'

'I don't know. What would I use? I don't know anything about poisons. She'd probably recover and have me arrested.'

'Not with what I'd give you. I know plenty about poishons!'

Agnes got up as if to go.

'Maybe if you tell me all this again when you're sober. Come and see me tomorrow when you've slept it off.'

'Sure thing,' said Laurens, then he grinned, and took another swig of Jim Beam.

II

Augusta lay in her bed and stared moodily at the ceiling.

'You bastard', she thought.

For thirty-three years she'd been under the impression that she'd had at least one man faithful to her until death. Then, just because *she* couldn't face the idea of a scandal, he'd made her suffer all that time, thinking him down there, suffocating slowly, trying to kick the end out of the coffin, and thinking his last thoughts about his beloved wife. Didn't the man have any heart at all?

And Anne Harringay! Who the hell was she when she was out? Augusta couldn't recall Anne Harringay to save her life. Maybe she was one of those minor guests that tagged along with others to the balls in the old days. She couldn't be expected to remember them all. The bitch! And she'd left a husband, too. Augusta didn't remember him, either. In truth, Augusta had always been so tied up with the sense of her own importance that it was a wonder she could remember anyone.

She lay and tried to remember Indigo as he was, and found that her memories of him were rather vague as well. Were his eyes blue or grey - grey she thought. And he had a sort of sandy, no, reddish hair. She'd have to ask Frederick. He'd remember. He could remember everything.

How humiliating this was. She wished she'd never dug him up. It was only stupid sentimentality after all, or was it?

Didn't she want to see how he'd struggled in the coffin, torn his hair out in clumps, kicked and screamed and clawed his eyes out, died with a look of horror on his face. Yes, that too! If he was stupid enough to crawl into an empty coffin and fall asleep, then he deserved all he got.

But he hadn't crawled into an empty coffin, had he? He'd planned it. Even down to the fifteen bricks.

The most awful thought was that in his hideaway he would have learnt that she didn't dig him up, but had a mock burial for him three days later. What a bitch he must think she was! How unfair! After all it was his fault, not hers. She wasn't to know that he was really running away, and that the coffin was empty, or she would have had to not dig it up again anyway. It was all so confusing.

At three o'clock she summoned Frederick, who came in and stood by her bed.

'Did you know about this, Frederick? Did you know that the coffin was empty?'

'Empty, Madam. I don't understand!'

'The coffin was empty, Frederick. Mr. Indigo ran away. He left a note for me, and fifteen bricks.'

147

'Well, the lord be praised,' said Frederick, smiling. 'That is good news, ma'am.'

'Good news? Good news, Frederick? How do you work that out?'

'Well it means that he lived, Miss Augusta. Here we've been thinking for thirty- three years that he died a horrible death, and it turns out that he didn't. Bravo, Mr. Indigo!'

'I would have thought, Frederick, that your first loyalty was to me. The least he could have done was what we thought he'd done, if only to justify those thirty-three years of suffering we've had to put up with.'

'Oh; I see, madam. You're saying that he should have done the decent thing, and died!'

'That's exactly right, Frederick. Instead, he left me to worry about whether to dig him up or not, the threat of scandal hanging over my head, then went off and had a good time with this Anne Harringay.'

'Anne Harringay, madam?'

'Yes. Anne Harringay. Do you remember an Anne Harringay, Frederick?'

'But of course, madam. She was the South wing under-parlourmaid. Her husband was the third reserve chauffeur. He only worked on Sundays, and filled in when the others were sick. He often drove you to church on a Sunday.'

'What - that dreadful little man with the peaked ears? Didn't he have a fling with Agnes once, at the Gordontown Races. In the back of the Benz, if I remember rightly.'

'That's correct, madam. You fired him after that.'

'Was that before or after his wife ran off with my husband?'

'The weekend before, if my memory serves me correctly, madam.'

'Well, what was she like, this under-parlourmaid?'

'The key word was 'under', madam. Under the houseboy, under the three chauffeurs, under the boots, under the weather most of the time, and under your husband!'

'Mostly under your husband, madam. She was a sprightly lass, if I remember, a twinkle in her eye, when she could get them open. Large buttocks, a slim waist, breasts that attempted to go in every direction except under her bra, madam. Surely you remember her. She served you breakfast in the mornings before going off to service your husband's appetite. While you were nibbling your toast, she was nibbling him.'

'For the life of me, I can't remember the girl. Was it so obvious, Frederick. Was I blind?'

'I'll put it this way. They once rolled past your doorway aboard the tea trolley, she squealing, and he pumping for all he was worth, and you didn't even look up from your paper, madam.'

Augusta sighed, and shook her head.

'I have been incredibly self-centred, haven't I, Frederick? So full of myself and my own importance that I have been blind to everyone else, even my husband and his needs. I should never have made him change his name at our wedding. That must have been most demeaning for him. Am I a bad person, Frederick?'

'Not bad, madam. Just rather stupid!'

'Thank you, Frederick. I suppose I was. Now leave me please, I have to sleep. I'll thank you not to mention this matter to either Agnes or Dr. Laurens.'

'I wouldn't think of it, madam.'

III

Edmund had been in touch with Eugenia to ask if it would be all right if Reginald's funeral was conducted slightly differently than the norm. At no extra cost to her they would be trying out a new device which would enable her grandchildren to see Reginald every so often, without him looking any different than he had in life. She was not in the best of moods, having just returned from an abortive visit to pastor Adam.

'Sure, you can do what you like with him. If he was silly enough to hang himself, then he can't really worry what happens to him now, can he?'

It was short and sweet. Edmund made arrangements to invite representatives from the senior citizens, the Old Folks Homes, meals on wheels, home care and the terminally ill association, not to mention the newly formed Seniors for Euthanasia. A short service was held in the chapel with no sign of a coffin at the altar. Afterwards, the party was led across to the gravesite, which by now had been completed and modified, even down to the headstone mounted already on top of the pyramided peak of the coffin, which just showed above ground.

Edmund had dressed Reginald in an overcoat, and placed the folds over his erection, his hands in the pockets. The overall look was rather debonair, as they had placed a hat at a rakish angle on Reginald's head, partly to hide the unnatural angle of his neck. The oldies gathered around the site, and Edmund made them stand back a way so that they would all be able to savour this first view of a Pepper Pop-up. Going to the pedestal, Edmund inserted the key, and waited a moment before giving it a twist.

'What you are about to see, ladies and gentlemen, is revolutionary in the art of burial. This is the first time in the world that this particular method has been used, though it won't be the last.'

'In the future, most of us will be interred in this manner, bringing a 'life to death' that we would never have thought possible. In the long distant future, your distant descendants may be able to come and visit you, and see what you actually looked like. If the process is followed correctly, a tape recording of your voice will accompany the presentation. If the widow, Mrs. Barry will please step forward, I give you - your husband.'

Edmund turned the key in the lock, and from the depths of the earth came the sound of a motor making contact. Then before their eyes, the headstone began to rise at a dignified speed into the air, followed by a square of perspex containing a man. His head became visible first, the hat raked, his colouring sublime. Then the shoulders; and the overcoat draped over him as the coffin gathered speed. It rose to about eight feet, and stopped with a thump. The sudden stop threw Reginald's head up and back, and his arms out wide. With them flew the overcoat, and Reginald stood shamelessly, flashing the audience with a huge erection.

There was a sharp intake of breath. The little old ladies put their hands over their mouths and looked perplexed. Then they all looked at each other for guidance, and hesitantly at first, someone at the back began to clap. Suddenly they were all clapping, and the women were laughing and whistling, the men making baudy comments at the size of his docker.

Edmund looked around and went white as a ghost. Eugenia stared fascinated at it, and started babbling in some strange tongue, known only to herself. An old man at the back said: 'I wanna be buried with one of those. You never know when you might need it!'

Everyone cracked up, and Edmund took the opportunity to slip Reginald back into the ground.

'That's the most original idea we've ever seen,' said one woman with a dark moustache. 'Are they all going to be like that?'

Edmund looked slightly green at this stage. He wore an apologetic grin, and nodded in a sickly fashion at the audience.

'Just teething problems,' he muttered, and closed the proceedings.

IV

Eugenia Barry had been caught badly off-guard by her husband's pop-up. As his head rolled back and stared directly at her, his voice in her head shouted: 'She did it! She did it! She hanged me, and broke my neck!'

She was horror-stricken, not knowing if everyone else had heard this accusation. Then she was hypnotized by that awful one-eyed creature, pointing straight at her and saying, in a deep, baritone voice: 'It was her - Eugenia Barry! She's guilty - guilty - guilty!' That's when she began to babble.

After all the hilarity had died down, she was led off and given a cup of tea by one old lady, who said, without any seeming relevance to anything: 'If he was mine, I'd have done the same thing, ducks.' Eugenia flung down her tea and fled.

Three minutes later she was beating tearfully on the Pastor's door, but he was hiding in his warren, and he wasn't answering the door to anyone. Brindy's remarks had stung him to the quick, and he was curled up in a ball on his bed, trying to think of ways of getting his own back. Suddenly he wasn't in love any more. He was in hate. What a bitch!

It hadn't occurred to him that she might not be seeking anything other than what she stated, which was a cure for the tumour. The fact that she had complied with his sexual demands so easily had led him into false pathways, and now he would have to extricate himself without appearing to lose face. He was angry at having allowed himself to slip into the trap, and he was furious at her for being so matter-of-fact about her own needs and requirements. In the meantime he lay in a funk on his bed, curled up in a foetal position.

Eugenia wasn't going to take no for an answer either. She tried the door and found it unlocked, so she walked in, and went directly to his living area.

'Oh pastor Adam, I'm sorry to disturb you, but I needed to talk to you badly. I've just been to my husband's funeral, and I've got a confession to make.'

Adam sat up, thinking he may as well make the best of it.

'What's that, Eugenia?'

He sighed, and made space for her to sit down.

'I killed my husband! Yes, I did! I thought that he might mess up our little group, so when he was hanging himself in the bedroom, I took the chair away. Then I boosted him up a couple of feet and let

155

him fall. It broke his neck. I need forgiveness, Adam. I need some sort of absolution.'

'We're not Catholics here,' said Adam. 'We don't do that sort of thing. Maybe you should go to the police and confess.'

Eugenia looked at him in fear.

'No, Adam, they'll lock me up. I'll go to prison and I'll never get out again. Surely you can just say a little prayer for me. I didn't mean it! I was just in a bad mood. I get like that sometimes. Maybe it was PMT?'

'I shouldn't imagine that you've suffered from PMT for ten years or more, Eugenia. Come on, be honest.'

'True. But sometimes it can come back, years later - can't it?'

'No, Eugenia. No it can't. If that's what you did, then that's what you're going to have to live with. I don't know that I can just not tell the police what you've told me, though. It's asking a lot.'

Eugenia looked alarmed.

'I thought everything in the confessional was sacred, that you were bound by a holy oath or something.'

'You're thinking of the Catholics. I'm not a Catholic priest, and that confession was not given in a confessional. I'm a lay preacher, which means that I made myself a priest, basically.'

Adam saw the look of fear and confusion in her face, and smiled. He was back in familiar territory.

'I'll do anything, Adam, anything. Don't let me go to jail.'

Adam paced the floor as if struggling with his conscience.

'I don't know, Eugenia; I really don't. I mean murder is murder! It's not like a little bit of shoplifting. If I don't tell, and they find out....'

'I'd never say a thing, Pastor Adam. Reeeally,' she wailed.

'There would have to be some sort of true penitence; a payment into church funds for instance. How much money can you come up with?'

Eugenia nearly choked.

'Money! I'm a poor widow, Adam...'

'What about your husband's insurance? I can find out, you know.'

Eugenia burst into tears and sat down heavily on the bed.

'I haven't got it yet. He had a life policy for $100,000. But they might not pay.'

'They'll pay,' said Adam, grimly. 'I suggest that you allot $60,000 to the flock. Make the cheque out to me, and I will see it's invested all right.'

'Sixty thousand dollars....' Eugenia spluttered, almost beside herself. 'That money was for my old age.'

'It would be no good to you in jail. In fact, if this comes out, they definitely won't pay you a penny. Forty thousand is better than nothing.'

'And you promise not to put me in!'

'I'll have to think about it,' he said, pacing again.

'One other thing; did you see that woman who came as you were leaving before?'

'Yes,' Eugenia said, sulkily. 'I suppose that's why you're treating me like this, because she's young and I'm not.'

'Not at all! That young woman has done me a lot of harm, and I need someone I can rely on to do something back to her.'

Eugenia brightened up at that. 'Really? I'll do it. I hate her.'

She thought of Brindy Somers, that youthful, elegant body, and was consumed with envy. This was her chance to get even.

'You don't even know her,' Adam said, wearily.

'I don't care. I hate her, and I'd do anything for you, Adam.'

'You'll do it to stop me telling the police what I know, that's why. From now on, Eugenia, I will be relying on you for all sorts of different things. You will do exactly what I say, when I say it, and never argue with me - is that clear?'

Eugenia moved closer to him, the light of a fanatic in her eye.

'I'll be your slave, Adam. I'll do anything you want me to do.'

'Anything?'

'Yes, anything,' she said.

Chapter Ten

Werner von Keppler had returned home, the gleam of fanaticism in his eyes. That suggestion by Edmund had his juices flowing. Sub-machine guns! What a great idea.

In his mind's eye he could see two coffins being spirited into parliament house, and in the middle of some boring debate about the use-by date of yogurt, the lids fly open and two corpses sit up and start spraying the chamber with machine-gun fire. It quite excited him. After all, what could they do? Charge the corpses? He walked around his little room chuckling to himself, and gathered the materials for the little job he had to do on Mrs. Bacon. Yes, he'd certainly have to keep that one in mind for a future project.

Edmund was busy making incisions into Mrs. Bacon's carotid artery and the femoral vein in her groin. He was remembering Mr. Bacon, a mincing little man who crooked his little finger when holding his teacup. He'd been a bit sus, Edmund thought.

A couple of years previously he'd fallen under a train, and had been split in half, fair up the middle. It was a hell of a thing getting his funeral clothes on because they'd had to sew him back together, and everything on the left was slightly out of place to everything on the right. His shoulders were lopsided, and they just about had to pour him into the coffin. Then his arms bunched up because the coffin was too narrow, so Edmund had finally decided to amputate the arms so he could lie flat. Once the arms were off, he cut them again at the elbow, slid the lower parts into the sleeves and crossed them across his chest.

That would have been fine, in fact it looked all right, you wouldn't have picked the problem just by a casual glance. But little Jason Bacon, his grandson, who was all of four, went up to the coffin to say goodbye to grandad, and wouldn't let go of his hand. It was twenty minutes before someone noticed little Jason was wandering around the parlour dragging a severed arm behind him.

The congregation scattered in horror, and Emlyn Jones chased him around the room and outside, trying to get him to give it up. But Jason was determined. He had Grandad's hand, and wasn't going to let it go.

Suddenly a huge rottweiler appeared from

nowhere, snatched the arm and took off. Dinner! The dog was spotted in various places over the next few days, but the arm was never seen again. Edmund shuddered at the memory. His father had almost had a seizure.

Once he'd finished pumping the formaldehyde solution into Mrs. Bacon, he rolled her over and attached a specially designed hinged bracket to her back, arms and shoulders. Werner had supplied this, and told him how to fit it. Then he took a piece of whalebone, curved at right angles, and carefully slid this down her throat and into the abdominal cavity. It had the desired effect, though made it a bit awkward for Brindy to make her up, as the corpse now lay with its legs up in the air. Nevertheless, they got through that stage between them, and dressed her in a nice green gown with long harlequin sleeves, which effectively hid the bracket from view. Then she was placed in the coffin, forced to lie flat, and the lid closed. She was to be a standard burial, not a pop-up, but that didn't mean that they couldn't improvise.

Edmund called the local television station and advised them that they should have their cameras at the service, because otherwise they would miss the next great leap forward in high-tech funerals.

He did the same with the radio station, and he also phoned a few local celebrities to invite them to attend. Then he left Brindy to it, and went home.

The moment Edmund disappeared, a tormented Dr. Carstairs staggered in and sat down, facing Brindy. She took one look at him, and groaned.

'Not now, Richard. Can't you see I've got my hands full at the moment.'

All Richard could see was Mrs. Bacon's undercarriage as he sat at the foot of the table, and she lay on her back with her legs in the air.

'Couldn't you wait until rigor mortis has subsided. That's disgusting,' he said.

'It's not rigor mortis, Richard. It's some new scheme Edmund's got. Something about high-tech funerals. I don't worry my head about such things. I just do my job.'

'I had to see you,' Richard went on, peering at her through Mrs. Bacon's legs. 'I can't go on without you. You're driving me crazy, Brindy. Can't we talk about this?'

'Not now, not ever. I made my decision, and I'm sticking to it.'

'But why? What difference does a tumour

make to our relationship? If you didn't have the tumour, we'd still be together.'

Brindy stopped and put down her brush.

'If you can't see what difference a terminal tumour makes to a relationship, then I suggest you get yourself a good psychiatrist. Whichever way you look at it, it spells *finis - end - goodbye!'*

'Okay, okay... what if this thing with your scumbag Pastor works. What then? Do we get back together?'

'No, Richard. We don't. I find it hard explaining to you, because you don't seem to grasp the obvious - or at least, what's obvious to me.'

'Well, what's that?' Richard scratched his head in frustration.

'See! You don't get it! How can I explain? You hand me a death warrant, then if that's not bad enough, you expect me to reconcile myself to it without putting up a fight. You say you'll stand by me to the end - I don't want someone standing by me, I want someone to do something about it.'

'But there's nothing to be done,' moaned Richard, at the end of his tether.

'There you go again, undermining me, trying to destroy my determination to beat this thing. Someone once said: 'If you can't say something nice, say nothing at all.' That's how I feel about you. Just say nothing at all. It would be more positive than what you've said up to this point.'

'That means you want me to lie to you. You want me to go against all the medical text books and lie to you, just so you can feel better.'

'Well, at least that would be a plus.'

'All right, I'll lie to you. You're going to be all right.'

'That's a lie, and you know it.'

Richard looked at her in confusion.

'Of course it's a lie. You just told me to lie!'

'So how can I trust you if you're going to lie to me all the time? If you can't make it at least sound like the truth, then you're wasting my time.'

'Okay...okay! I give up. I just need your signature on this piece of paper, and I'll leave you in peace.'

'My signature for what? Oh, you want me to leave you my CD Collection. If I die, it's yours. Now will you go away?'

'No, this is nothing to do with your CD Collection. It's you I want.'

'Richard, we've just been all over this. It's over! Finished! Get out of my life!'

'No, I mean I want you when you're dead. I'll

need your signature, here, and that will give me the necessary authority.'

Brindy stopped, and frowned.

'What authority - when I'm *dead!* What on earth are you babbling about, Richard?'

'I want to have you embalmed, then I can take you home with me.' Richard had a pleading look in his eye, but Brindy was just taken aback.

'Embalmed! You want to take me home with you? You have got to be kidding.'

'Well it won't matter to you - you'll be dead. And I'll look after you my pet; I'll keep fresh flowers by you always and keep you in the shade, where you can look out on the garden. I'll even put a shawl around you in the winter.'

'Oh yes, and stick your fingers up my dress when I can't defend myself. Ask your friends in for a night's cards, and let me sit in. Of course, I won't be able to play; I'll be dead. But I'm sure I would be a great talking point. You could even strip me off, and use me for your biology classes - gee, I'd like that! Piss off, Richard. If I die, I'm going to be buried like everyone else.'

'I can't see that what I'm asking is so terrible. You'll be shedding your skin, I will be picking it up and cherishing it.'

'You will be doing nothing of the sort. I am

not yours, alive or dead. Do you get that? Now get out of here before I have you arrested, you pervert.'

Richard stalked out, bitter, but still determined.

II

Joanne couldn't wait to get back to the South Wing. She'd mentally kicked herself for getting spooked the last time she was there, and wished she'd continued going through the maps and documentation instead of sitting there like a first class idiot, waiting for footsteps. Once her chores were done she slipped out the back way and headed for her usual access point, stopping along the way to sit on a bench in the sun, mainly to see if she was being followed. After ten minutes of watchfulness she judged it safe to continue, and made her way through the weeds to the rear door. It was open

She stopped dead at this. She always closed the door after her, it was automatic. Someone else had either been there, or was in the Wing at this very moment. She almost turned and fled, but she so much wanted to get back to that room that her foolhardiness overcame her fear. She stepped quietly inside, looking for footprints on the floor. There was nothing so obvious, and she relaxed a little. It was eerie, walking along those passageways, expecting to bump into the unknown at any moment. She got to the ballroom, and looked around carefully before exposing herself to its great expanse.

Tripping across, once she thought it safe, she was shortly in the passageway behind and forcing her way into the small study. She breathed a sigh of relief as she shut the door behind her, and sank down in the chair at the desk.

Everything was just as she'd left it. She pulled out a couple of the maps, determined to see them all so that in her own mind she could catalogue all that they contained.

She put the first few aside, they held nothing new for her. The next was the plan for the North wing, the most recent addition, dated 1914. There was not a lot of interest there. Next she pulled out the South wing plans of 1892, and she could identify most of the ground floor rooms from this, including the one she was sitting in behind the ballroom. It was marked on the map as a broom closet, and that was probably what it was, originally. Later, one of the owners must have felt it would serve as a good spot to do a bit of paperwork, and had it upgraded with the desk and pigeonholes. That might have been in the '20's.

Then there was another plan of the South wing, dated 1890, but this only showed an outline of where the Wing would stand once it was built. Most of the features on the map were topographical, showing the features of the ground. Just outside the most southerly section of the building was a round depression in the land, or hole. An arrow marked this as 'B' Shaft, Coverleigh Mine. She'd known there was mining in the area, but she didn't realize it had been this close. A shaft, just on the perimeter of the building. Other markings tended to indicate the direction of tunnels running from the shaft, and one of these pointed towards the future position of the ballroom.

The next map was a map of the Coverleigh Mine, showing levels and drives and giving accurate assessments of the lodes found there. It had been a copper mine, and the tunnels ran off on an east-west axis, with some smaller tunnels headed off at right angles, though not very far. They had obviously followed a vein of ore, and this had run straight through the present cemetery. What interested Joanne was the tunnel that ran underneath the ballroom from the shaft at the end of the building. She wondered if they had filled that in before building?

The following map was a very old map of the cemetery, dated 1870, and on this, besides the few plots that had already been taken up, there were several family vaults, and an area marked as 'catacombs'. The entry to these appeared to have been built over by the Varley family when they erected their family vault, but there was a tunnel leading off in an easterly direction from these though the end of the tunnel wasn't shown.

Joanne delved into the pile, and found another map of the South Wing, one dated 1904. This was a map showing the location of cellars in the building for the storing of wine and food. The wine cellar was north of the ballroom, and accessible through a pantry off the kitchen. There was a large meat-hanging cellar close to this, accessible via the wine cellar, and also from the other end of the kitchen itself. There must have been a trapdoor down to this. The third cellar was marked, but there was no indication what it was for. This was southeast of the ballroom, and accessible from a master bedroom in that section. She took a mental note of the room number, and determined to explore that avenue later.

Looking at the time, Joanne put the maps

back, and slipped out of the room, closing the door behind her. She intended exiting by the ballroom front entrance so she could walk around and see where this old shaft had been. As she made her way into the ballroom, and headed for the double doors, she suddenly heard noises in the building, muffled, but like a man, talking to himself. She stopped and listened. Nothing!

Joanne hurried to the door, and let herself out. She walked around to the south side of the building looking for the mineshaft, but all she found were the remains of a rock garden with a pathway between that and the house. Everything was totally overgrown and neglected, and although she searched for signs of old diggings, there was nothing that struck her as obvious. She made her way along the rear of the house and closed the door she had entered by, and then returned to the Great Hall.

III

The following day had all the auspices of a great day for the town of Port Waterdale. There were two television crews roaming the town, looking for extra footage for fill-ins if this funeral turned out to be a fizzer.

Channel 6 interviewed an old lady stuck in the mud by the racecourse, and bombarded her with questions about the local council, the state of the roads, help for the aged and how was she coping on the old age pension, before leaving in a rush to interview a performing seal near the jetty, leaving her still stuck in the mud.

Channel 8VTO FRT PW, the local channel, interviewed the publican of the 'Horse & Monkey' about how lucrative the slot machines were, and did he think they should have been made available only to sporting clubs. This while they downed nine pints each, with whiskey chasers.

Werner had been tied up in the chapel all morning with Mrs. Bacon, screwing, soldering, testing, adjusting until he was satisfied that nothing would go amiss. Jonathon Pepper had been hovering nervously in the background, taking note of the rising interest in the town, and praying long and deeply. He couldn't stand another stuff-up like Reginald Barry. He was looking old, even for his 66 years. This experimental period was very trying on his nerves.

At least Reginald Barry had been fixed. He would never flash anyone again, Jonathon had seen to that. The next morning he had popped Reg up, opened the front of the coffin and permanently attached the overcoat so it could never fly open again. He did this with the simple expedient of a very large safety pin, pushed through the coat on one side, and Reginald's alter ego on the other. Reg now had a safety pin through his dick.

At one o'clock sharp the people began to pour into the little Church of the Ascension in Bright Street, Mrs. Bacon's own church, to find two camera crews and their cameras already in place.

Once the congregation was settled, the pallbearers appeared with the coffin, and this was placed at the right hand side at the front, elevated somewhat and to the side of the altar. Werner von Keppler hid behind a column holding a little controller, similar to a model aircraft guidance device. Jonathon and Edmund stood at the back where half of the town was gathered out of curiosity.

The vicar had only just returned from a holiday in Portugal, and was almost late for the service himself. He dashed in the side door at the last minute, and composed himself as he walked in and genuflected at the altar.

The service was read, and everything seemed

very straightforward and boring to the camera crews, who muttered amongst themselves, as the vicar's voice droned on. Then came the part where the choir was going to sing some of Mrs. Bacon's favourite hymns. As the local music teacher she had taught most of these lads, and they now lined up in front of her coffin to give her a right royal send-off. The vicar announced the first hymn – 'Hark! The Herald Angels Sing.' Everyone stood up.

Almost imperceptibly at first the coffin lid began to rise. It opened up fully within about twenty seconds, by which time the organist was playing the introduction, and everyone else was standing, paralyzed, watching the coffin.

Suddenly Mrs. Bacon sat straight up, stared at the congregation, lifted a baton in the air and rapped twice on the side of her coffin. She then nodded her head once, and began to conduct the hymn, keeping perfect time with the organist, who was totally unaware of this turn of events. She had her back to the congregation, and could only go by the sheet music in front of her.

The front three rows turned as white as a sheet. The choir came to a strangled silence as their hair stood collectively up on end. The vicar staggered back three paces holding his throat, and those at the back formed a bottleneck as they fought each other to get out of the church first.

Suddenly there was chaos and confusion, and the camera crews were feverishly filming this turn of events, while trying to look as unobtrusive as possible.

The vicar dashed over and grabbed a container, filling it with holy water from the font, and returned to fling it in the face of this devil's work. Mrs. Bacon turned her head at this slight, stopped conducting, raised her other hand out of the coffin, held it up on high and fired two shots into the ceiling from a Smith & Wesson revolver. The vicar let out a howl of terror and hid behind the altar, the rush at the back halted, and those who were left returned to their seats, hands in the air.

Mrs. Bacon rapped smartly on the side of her coffin with the baton, and the organist looked around, let out a huge fart, and fell off the stool. The choir got everyone started on 'Hark! The Herald Angels Sing', and the congregation joined in, and all the while the cameras rolled while the corpse conducted her own funeral service.

After the service it was bedlam outside while the two funeral directors tried to explain that they hadn't had time to brief the vicar as he'd been late in getting back, and Edmund collared Werner as he was slinking away to ask him about the revolver. It seemed he'd taken to Edmund's suggestion so much that he'd tried to get hold of a sub-machine gun. But the best he could do was a revolver. They managed to pass that off as a bit of cowboy extravagance, and once the vicar had calmed down, they promised to repair the bullet holes in his roof.

The six o'clock news that night was viewed by a record audience. Mrs. Bacon became more famous in death than she could have dreamed of in life. Suddenly Pepper's Funerals was a national icon, and the phone began to ring with offers to franchise. The local constable made a quiet call on Werner to warn him about weapons violations, but all in all it was a howling success. The only downside that anyone could see was that during the service three people, including a cameraman's sideboy, died of heart attacks, and one old lady had a stroke.

Chapter Eleven

James Coverleigh was not happy about his rival's publicity, not happy at all. After all the work he'd done trying to convince people that going underground was not the way of the future, Edmund had shown that it was. His phone rang that morning, not with new business, but with cancellations for business he'd already written.

James had never felt the need to take a defensive posture, and he didn't feel the need for it now. He would go on the attack. If Edmund could use robotics to his advantage, then he could too.

He picked up the phone and called Sam Everton at Systems Evaluations PLC, and asked for a representative to call. He was not going to be out-technologised by a couple of amateurs. Valhalla had cost an arm and a leg to develop, and it was imperative that it showed a constant and continuous return on investment. The bank alone would demand that, and he needed the continuing support of the bank.

A young whizz-kid by the name of Andrei Sikorny was sent out immediately to give

Valhalla the once over. The company had already done their homework, watching news tapes of Edmund's propaganda, so they had a pretty good idea what James would be expecting. Andrei got the red carpet treatment, and a personal viewing of all the systems currently in place. James took him around personally.

'Very impressive! The automatic stacking and coffin shuffling system is first rate,' said Andrei, who had never seen a facility like this before. 'I also like Gabriel, even though he belongs to the opposition. He's very suitable for your particular application. What do you require from us though, that's the question?'

'We're going to have to delve more deeply into robotics,' said James. 'You saw that blasted music teacher, conducting her own funeral? Well, it was a great publicity stunt, and it's damaged us. You see, although we offer people all those things they've been brought up to believe is their right after death; heaven, hell, purgatory, our corpses are nevertheless inanimate. They just lie there and accept passively what is offered to them. We have to beat a bit of life back into them if we're going to compete in the popular marketplace.'

'You want to go interactive in other words.'

'Yes, We want people to see that they can do the same things they've always done, ad infinitum, especially in hell, where all the popular culture really exists. If some old biddy was in the habit of going down the rubbidy-dub every Saturday and playing the pokies, then she should be able to continue that in 'HELL'. We need to install a system that gets them from the coffin to the poker machine, or even *in* the coffin to the poker machine, where they will be close enough to be able to reach out and push the buttons.'

'We could even make this a fair dinkhum sort of gaming venue where the rellies put in a few bucks for the old dear to gamble away each month. Any wins would automatically come off their monthly payments, so the activity would affect the world of the living as well as show some desirable after-death activity. It has to be better than some once-only 'conducting the funeral service' kind of thing. That's all very well, but people will soon see the limitations. No, we need regular activities to keep our corpses occupied.'

'So basically we're looking at animating the corpses to do one or more of the activities that they enjoyed in life.'

'That's right. There will be a cost factor, of course, and this will be borne by their estate, or by the relatives. The more activities, the greater the cost.'

'Just how stable are these corpses? Are they likely to fall apart if they pursue, say, a rigorous exercise?' said Andrei, speculatively.

'Well, obviously, they won't be playing rugby, or sunning themselves under ultra violet lights. But apart from those types of damaging activities, the skin is soft and pliable, something like leather, and the bone structure, well, depends on whether they had arthritis or not. I suppose, in special circumstances, and given an additional cost factor, we could have the bones scraped and wired and replaced, giving them a whole new lease of... death!'

'Fascinating,' commented Andrei. 'What about more personal pursuits, you know....'

'Well, they can't exactly go visiting their friends for a chat. That's hard one.'

'What about feeding people's hatreds. You know, the things they really detest about life.'

James rubbed his chin.

'You mean politicians and lawyers? True, we could have a shooting gallery where once a week they could pick off a politician of their time. We could use .22 calibre pistols, and the coffins could be mounted on a conveyor moving from side to side in front of the illustrations. That would give the pollies a sporting chance. Five shots each, then change coffins. That could become a national pastime.'

'As far as lawyers are concerned, we could have a mock-up court where the lawyer sits in the dock, and the people pronounce judgement. They could institute different penalties like sentencing them to be cremated, or driving a huge screw into their anus, pretty much the same way they screwed everybody else in life.'

'You realize what you are doing here, don't you,' said Andrei. 'You're re-vamping an entire industry. There will be increased employment, less reason to remain unemployed. A facility like this in every town could become the town's main employer. In fifty years you could be looking at fifty percent of the population living off a hundred per cent of the dead population. A case of you scratch my back, and I'll stop the skin flaking off yours.'

'Fantastic!' said James. 'And Valhalla will go down in history as the place where it all started. A bit like the Industrial revolution. Well, can you do it?'

'With our expertise and your ideas, Mr. Coverleigh, we certainly can,' smiled Andrei.

'We'll have our engineers in here tomorrow to start working on it. You'd better make a few corpses available for experimental work.'

James felt a whole lot better as he watched Andrei drive away.

II

Augusta snapped out of her mood on the third day, and took the car into town. Laurens offered to go with her – basically because he didn't trust her – but she waved away any offers of help.

'I'm quite capable of attending to my own affairs, William. I don't need a nursemaid. I shall do what I have to do, and will be back for dinner. Frederick, the car!'

Frederick drove the old Bentley out of the garage, and donned a chauffeur's hat. The family had no need of a chauffeur these days, but Frederick was a great one for keeping up appearances, and it wouldn't do to let the locals know that the family in the Great Hall were under any kind of necessity. He drove her to a seafront villa in Port Waterdale, which had been converted into the offices of Snipe, Partridge &

Game, Solicitors. The firm had been established in 1907, so there was no Snipe any more, and the last Partridge had fled the nest in 1956. There were however, a couple of Game's, and this, reflected Augusta, was pretty well the way the world had turned over the past few years.

On her imperious entry, the bimbo Joylene, who had hurriedly adjusted her dress, shuffled some papers industriously on her desk, and announced that Mr. Game would be with her shortly. In actual fact, Mr. Game had seen the Bentley pull up, and was hiding out the back, hoping to hear what she wanted before making his entrance.

Augusta was ushered into his office, and took a seat opposite him. She laid her bag on his desk.

'To business, Mr. Game. I wish you to inform me of the full extent of the family fortune, listing everything from real property to investments and income.'

'Certainly, Mrs. Branwood. It will take some time of course, I should be able to have the figures in a couple of days.'

'You have five minutes, Mr. Game. You may inform me as you go. If you need to make a few phone calls, I'm quite prepared to wait.'

Augusta stared him down, and Lawrence

Game shifted awkwardly in his seat. Suddenly he felt his tie was choking him, so he loosened it.

'I can give you some figures, of course....'

'I can be very patient when I want. If this takes us through your lunch hour Mr. Game, then so be it. Let us commence.'

The next hour or so Augusta made copious notes in a little black book she carried in her bag. The house and land, it seemed, was now worth somewhere in the region of six million dollars. Some of this could be commuted if the family were prepared to divest themselves of some of the land for a building estate. Augusta just hmm'd at this suggestion.

The furniture was insured for $800,000, but a lot of that depended on the original antiques still being maintained in good order. In the banks, spread over seven different accounts, there was a sum of.... $342,763; plus or minus the expenses of the moment, and interest.

Stocks and shares were more complicated. The dividends had varied widely over the past couple of years, though her bank shares and Telstra were on a high. To all intents and purposes, the original capital had grown to about 2.7 million dollars under her strict regime, and could very well peak at $3m within seven years.

Augusta raised her eyebrows at this, but made no comment.

There were other sundry direct investments in local businesses that amounted to approximately $430,000, and her only liability was the loan for Valhalla, which she had guaranteed, and that was running at approximately $380,000. She would be happy to know, however, that this loan was being repaid at an admirable rate, and could well be completed within three years.

Augusta slipped her little book back into her bag, and placed it on her lap.

'Thank you for your trouble, Mr. Game, I am indebted to you. Now what I want you to do is this. I want you to make out a number of cheques for me, and make them to the following people. James Coverleigh - $50,000. Are you getting this?'

Lawrence nodded, hurriedly.

'Agnes Coverleigh, $40,000. Frederick Varley, $35,000. Emily Cherry, $20,000. Dr. William Laurens, $50,000. Joanne Destry, $10,000. And that's it! I would like those cheques to be delivered to me, personally, in one week's time. I will sign them then.'

Augusta got up to leave. As she passed through the outer office, she made a detour to where Joylene sat at her desk. With a knowing look at the 'secretary', she tossed her head and stalked through the door.

III

Agnes was daydreaming in her coffin when Dr. Laurens burst in, quite sober this time but looking extremely harrassed.

'Put that thing away, Agnes, it's past its use-by date.'

He paced the room as she clambered in confusion out of her coffin, shaken out of her dream of large hairy men.

'Doesn't anyone in this house believe in knocking?' Agnes exclaimed, angrily. 'I shall have to start bolting my door.'

'Listen, Agnes, this is serious! Are you going to do what we talked about the other day, or not? I tell you, Augusta has been to see her solicitors, and it doesn't look good. The longer we delay, the harder it's going to be.'

'You were supposed to come and talk to me when you were sober,' Agnes said, sternly. 'You've had plenty of opportunity – where have you been?'

'I didn't want to be so obvious. I thought I'd

wait until we wouldn't be seen together, but I think things are coming to a head. It's all the fault of that stupid husband of hers.'

'You mean Indigo? How could it be his fault? He's been buried for over thirty years.'

'Yes, but she dug him up. She got James and Frederick to dig him up the other night, and now she's gone all maudlin on me. She won't even talk to me about it. It's dragged the whole affair back into the open, and if the facts come out, I'm for the high jump.'

'I haven't got a clue what you're talking about, William,' said Agnes, puzzled.

'No, of course not. You were only in your twenties at the time, and there was only myself, Augusta, and I think Frederick who knew anything about it. The only other one was Benjamin Pepper, the funeral director, but I doubt if he ever told anyone. It would have been bad for business.'

Laurens continued pacing the floor, agitated.

'The fact is, Agnes, that Indigo wasn't dead. He got buried by mistake instead of Mark Daventry, and we only found out about it two days later. We could have dug him up, of course, but Augusta wouldn't have it at the time. She thought it would cause a scandal – which it would, of course. So they got me to make out a death certificate for Indigo, then buried Daventry in Indigo's grave the day after that. It was all hushed up.'

Agnes sat there stunned. Her mouth opened to speak, but no words would come. Finally, she said: 'You buried him *alive?*'

Laurens turned to her, and nodded.

'Blame your cousin. I was for digging him up. But you can see the spot it puts me in. If there's an investigation now, I'll end up disbarred, and will probably go to prison.'

'So that's what it's all about,' said Agnes, wonderingly. 'Fancy me not knowing, after all these years. And I was at both funerals, too.'

'I know you were. So were a lot of other people. We kept it very hush-hush.'

They were both silent for some time. Laurens sighed, and flopped into a chair.

'You know, I actually feel a bit better now, after being able to tell someone about it. It's plagued me for over thirty years. There hasn't been a day gone by that I don't see him, Indigo, waking up in that coffin, realizing that he's been buried, and that he's going to die in there. It's made me claustrophobic all my life. I can't abide closed-in places.'

'So you think that by bumping Augusta off, you'll be safe. What about me? I know now. Are you going to bump me off too?'

'It's only hearsay evidence as far as you're concerned. It wouldn't stand up in court. If they check his body now, what's left of it, they've got Buckley's chance of finding out what he died from. Probably accept a heart attack, though there wouldn't be enough left to prove anything like that. With Augusta though, it's different. As she said, with her it was an accident. With me it was collusion, conspiracy, the breaking of my Hippocratic oath.'

'I see. Well, if you still want to do it, I'm game. I don't feel so exposed now that I've got something on you as well. We'll both have to just keep quiet about it, won't we?'

'I'm glad you understand at last. Right, I've brought this little gadget with me, with just the right stuff to do the trick.'

He pulled out a hypodermic syringe from his pocket, with a safety cap over the needle.

'You'll need to inject her where it won't be so obvious. Just a little bit of this will be enough to paralyze her completely, then once we've got her to that stage I'll spend some time alone with her and finish the job. No one will suspect. I'm a doctor, after all.'

'What is it exactly?' Agnes said, taking the hypodermic gingerly between thumb and forefinger.

'Probably better that you don't know. That way you can't say, can you.'

'Well, how long before it takes effect. If she wakes up and catches me, I don't want her running around the house screaming and making accusations before becoming paralyzed, do I?'

'Two to three minutes, maybe sooner. She'll lose the power of speech within about thirty seconds. She should be totally paralyzed within three minutes, though she will know exactly what's going on around her, and she will be totally conscious until the end. That's what's going to make it hard. Those eyes!'

Agnes put the hypodermic carefully away in her handbag. She then hid the handbag in a cupboard.

'Is there any chance that it'll wear off, that she'll become un-paralyzed before the end. I'd hate it if she started to come to while I was waiting for you.'

'No, there won't be any of that. If she did manage to survive, which she won't, she'd be a hopeless vegetable for the rest of her life.'

'We'll consider it a pact, then. A pact!'

Agnes looked excited for the first time. For once she was going to take her life into her own hands and do something to positively affect that life. She would finally come into her own.

'Call me the moment it's done,' said Laurens, letting himself out.

IV

Edmund and Jonathon were so busy over the next few days, fielding requests for franchises of their name and product, that they completely missed the television commercials which were going to blow a chill wind across their bows. James had wasted no time once the engineers moved in, and started changing things.

'This 'PURGATORY' is going to have to go,' said Mullins, the senior engineer. 'If we're going to have enough room for the new systems, 'HELL' is going to have to be greatly enlarged. 'PURGATORY' takes up a hundred yards of space, we're going to need about eighty of those to expand.'

James was nonplussed.

'We can't just get rid of 'PURGATORY', people expect it. They can't just go straight to

'HEAVEN' or 'HELL'. That's in the Bible! What if we shorten the time that they spend in 'PURGATORY'? Take it down to three and a half days. That way we might be able to get down to a couple of rows for those on their way up, or on their way down.'

'Two days,' said Mullins. 'Then you could get down to one row.'

'Impossible. We'd have to re-write the Bible! Christ spent three days there, so any ordinary person would have to spend more, it stands to reason.'

'What percentage of your income came from the Bible in the last financial year?' asked the engineer. James looked uncertain.

'Well, none – *directly!* But indirectly of course, you could say that all our income is derived from it. Without religion and burial rites, we'd be in Queer Street.'

'You're going to have to look long and hard at where your income is *directly* derived from. If that means trampling on a set of beliefs, well, that's the price we pay for dealing in the current marketplace. Think of it as just another Reformation. It was good enough for Henry VIII to change the rules – why not you?'

'True; there's a lot of sense in what you're

saying,' said James. 'Okay, what if we cut 'HEAVEN' down a bit, and incorporate 'PURGATORY' up that end?'

'Now you're talking! There doesn't seem to be a lot of activities mapped out for 'HEAVEN' anyway. Just a lot of praying and mumbling, and kneeling on mats. You'll never be able to fit enough harps in there for those who genuinely want to learn how to play them, so they're going to be disappointed anyway. They can't scourge themselves, because it will eventually wear the flesh off their backs, and sackcloth and ashes are too hard to clean up. That leaves hair shirts, but once fleas get into a building, they spread everywhere. It won't only be the saints who are scratching.'

'None of this looks too good for 'HEAVEN', does it?' mused James. 'No one wants an eternity of twiddling their thumbs. How are we going to make 'HEAVEN' the place to be, when all the action is going on down the other end?'

'It's a tough one,' agreed Mullins. 'Once you see how it goes, you might have to swap the names around – make 'HELL' into 'HEAVEN' and vice versa.'

'That's not so silly as it sounds. Sitting around and listening to harps all day, for eternity, would be most people's idea of hell anyway, and it would be one way of bringing the heathens into the church, wouldn't it? As a matter of fact, I think the ancient church pulled a stunt like that once, when they changed the day of worship from a Saturday to a Sunday. They used the same argument.'

In the end, a compromise was reached. 'HEAVEN' was to be cut down to fifty yards from its original hundred, while 'PURGATORY' was to be set in as an adjunct to 'HEAVEN', encroaching on fifteen yards of 'HEAVEN' on the front side, and extending only halfway across the building, then taking up fifteen yards of the new, enlarged 'HELL', whose rear boundary now would be conterminous with that of 'HEAVEN' on the far side of the building. The major activity of those in 'HEAVEN' would from henceforth be flying lessons, undertaken every Sunday on overhead wires with wings fitted. The only problem was that they might have to apply to the devil for airspace, as part of the route would be to fly over 'HELL'.

This meant that 'HELL' would be a massive two hundred and fifty yards long at the rear, and two hundred and thirty five feet along the front. This, of course, meant that the main doors, set in a hundred and fifty feet along the side wall of the building, would now open directly into 'HELL',

'We'll just have to make it that the only way to get to either 'HEAVEN' or 'PURGATORY' is via 'HELL',' said James. 'A bit hard for the purists to grasp, but we'll bring them around in the end.'

The television ads began on Channel 6. A couple was shown lying in bed, caressing each other, about to make love. The voice-over said:

'Just another loving couple, delighting in the sensuality of their bodies, embarking on the fruits of love. But this couple is different. You see, these two are dead! That's right, ladies and gentlemen, these happy corpses are just two of the contented cadavers now housed in Valhalla, the death house that makes light of life. After all, why should you have to give up a healthy sensual life, just because you're dead? With Valhalla's specially planned afterdeath, you will have a packed timetable of favourite pastimes to keep you occupied for eternity. Join the happy throng – book your coffin now!'

Another one ran:

'See this old lady following her favourite pastime, playing the pokies. She wins some, she loses some, but she gets a great kick out of it nevertheless. The one advantage she has over you punters out there is that she'll never age another day. That's right folks, not one day! Is that because of some strange effect of playing this particular machine. Not at all! This lady will never age, because she's already dead! I'll tell you something else, as well. This lady's wins contribute to her upkeep at Valhalla, freeing family finances for other uses. Phone Valhalla today, and book your grandma a pokie.'

Or: *'Euthanasia knocks, ladies and gentlemen. The legislation is through, and the baby boomers are heading over the hill. If you have a baby boomer in your household, tying up a perfectly useful bedroom, or driving you crazy with their old rock 'n roll records, maybe we can help. Book an interview today at Valhalla, and you'll be surprised at the scope of our remedies. We have a wide range of terminations, certainly one that will suit your pocket. (Conditions Apply!).'*

Chapter Twelve

Brindy Somers headed out to the old church, checking carefully as she went that she wasn't being followed. Richard's behaviour over the past week was making her paranoid, and she was beginning to imagine him behind every tree. She put her head down and hurried so that she could get safely inside before being accosted.

She'd been feeling pretty positive about the tumour for the past few days, as her vision had returned to normal, the headaches had gone, and her balance was restored. She was feeling fit and well, and found it hard to believe that she was still under sentence of death.

She knocked on the door, and pastor Adam answered, looking none too happy today. But he ushered her inside, and they continued through to his living area. There she sat down on his bed, and matter-of-factly kicked off her shoes, and peeled off her panty-hose.

'What's the problem, Adam?' she asked, as he sat there, watching her. 'You look different today. Are we going to do this, or what?'

'We have a slightly different schedule for today,' Adam replied, coldly. 'The rules of the game have changed.'

Brindy looked at him, puzzled.

'Is this anything to do with what I said to you the other day?' she said. 'I'm surprised at you, Adam. You're supposed to be a man of God, doing his works. The idea of all this was to help me get rid of this tumour, not to win yourself another girlfriend.'

'You hurt me severely,' said Adam. 'You cut me to the quick.'

'Well, I'm sorry about that, but I tend to speak my mind. I haven't got time to play footsie with people. You forget what sort of a timetable I'm on.'

'*You* forget that when someone offers you love, you don't gouge out their eyes. You really went over the top.'

Brindy sighed.

'Look. This is getting us nowhere. Today's obviously not convenient for you, so I'll give it a miss. Maybe I'll catch up with you at some other time.'

'Oh no! I have a schedule for you, it's just probably not one that you'll like.' Adam looked quite mean at this point. Brindy began to feel apprehensive.

'Look, I'm going. I'll see you later.'

'No you're not,' said a voice behind her. 'You're not going anywhere.'

Brindy looked around and saw Eugenia Barry pointing a gun at her head. Adam looked at her, and grinned.

'You get the drift?' he said. 'Put your hands behind your back.'

'You can't do this! Have you two gone mad?'

'Just do it, or it will be the worse for you,' Eugenia snapped. 'I'm not afraid to use this thing.'

Brindy put her hands behind her back, and Adam tied them together with twine. He did a good job of it, looping several strands tightly around so that she was pinioned fast.

'This is going to look good on your record. Kidnapping, unlawfully detaining me against my will...'

'Shut your mouth,' said Eugenia, slapping her hard around the face.

'Come on,' said Adam, dragging her off the bed by the hair. 'You're going to have to do penance. I've got the perfect place for you.'

He pushed her in front of him to the rear of the building, and into a small antechamber. There he pulled up a trapdoor in the floor, revealing some wooden steps downwards. He pushed her ahead of him, and they began to descend. At the bottom, it took some getting used to the gloom, but Adam lit a torch and Brindy saw that they were in a tunnel of some kind, a long tunnel that ran off into the distance with no light at the end. He pushed her ahead of him and they kept walking for what must have been a hundred metres or more. At this point the tunnel branched into two, and they took the left-hand branch. Thirty metres further on it branched again, but one side it was only a cutting, about ten metres long. At the end of that there was a rough stairway upwards, apparently leading nowhere.

Adam went up first and pulled on an old, rusty lever. A stone moved aside, like a marble slab, and he beckoned her up the steps. Once there, he pushed her through the gap ahead of him, and she climbed out into a dark room, filled with boxes piled on top of each other.

Eugenia followed them up, and they stood there, in the gloom.

'Now I'm going to give you a lesson in manners,' said Adam. 'You've put me through a lot of pain during the last few days. I'm going to give you some solitary time to think over what you said, and then I'll come back. When I do, I want to hear an apology. I want to hear you say – 'I love you, Adam', because you know you do.'

'Now look here. I don't know who you think you are, but you can let me go this minute, do you hear. I've got no intention of doing penance for anything, for you, or for anybody.'

'You have no intention....' sneered Adam. 'Lady, you have no choice. Get in there.' He indicated a long box on the floor, its lid open. Brindy's eyes finally made out what it was – a coffin.

She looked around the room; coffins, all stacked up neatly on top of each other. Between them Adam and Eugenia manhandled her into the coffin and held her down. Then Adam rolled her half over and cut the cord on her wrists. Before she could move, he had dropped the lid, and thrown a bolt over on the outside. She was locked in. She could still see them as there had been a circle cut out of the lid, just level with her face. But the rest of her couldn't move, she was so tightly fitted in.

'Get me out of here, Adam. You just get me out of here or I'll scream.'

'You can scream to your heart's content, dear,' said Eugenia, sweetly. 'No one can hear you in here. You're in a marble vault, with walls two feet thick. The last burial here was in 1957. That's how long it's been since those oak doors were opened.'

'You can't be serious,' said Brindy, panicking. 'Look, a joke's a joke. Let me out of here, you've had your fun.'

'We'll see how you feel tomorrow. Perhaps you'll be in a more penitent frame of mind,' said Adam. 'In the meantime, we just have one other thing to do.'

He and Eugenia picked up another coffin that was fitted with four short legs, and stood it on top of the one Brindy was in. Suddenly she couldn't see a thing, though there was still an airspace between the two coffins. She could still hear their voices.

'You now have the body of a man on top of you who has been dead for a hundred and twenty nine years,' she heard Adam say. 'Enjoy!'

The two let themselves out, and she heard the marble slab slide back into place. Suddenly there was a deathly silence. All Brindy could feel was the terror rising in her throat.

II

Agnes waited until nightfall, then took her bag out of the cupboard and retrieved the hypodermic syringe. She placed it in the pocket of her cardigan and wandered out into the dining room to see how many others were about. Dinner was still being served, and Joanne Destry was at the table with Augusta, but Frederick was nowhere to be seen. Agnes sat down and rang the little bell, and shortly Mrs. Cherry came out with her plate.

'I'll be off, if that's all right with you, Miss Augusta. I'll deal with the dishes in the morning.'

'Certainly Emily, there's no reason to hold you back.'

Augusta was the essence of good humour this evening.

'Oh, by the way; has anyone seen Dr. Laurens about the place? He disappeared this afternoon, and I need to speak with him.'

'He did put his head in and say he wouldn't be eating tonight,' said Mrs. Cherry.

'Oh? When was that?'

'About an hour ago, Miss Augusta. He didn't say why.'

Agnes looked down at her plate, and kept eating. What was he playing at now? How was she supposed to get in touch with him if he was going to keep disappearing all the time?

Joanne finished her food and got up from the table.

'I think I might have an early night. I'm very tired for some reason.'

Augusta nodded at her, and she left the room.

'You're very quiet tonight, Agnes. Something got your tongue?'

Agnes looked up, guiltily. She could feel the syringe in her pocket, but could not see any immediate chance of using it. She realized she'd have to speak.

'I was just thinking about Mrs. Bacon, that funeral, you know. The things they can do in this day and age. It makes me feel quite old.'

'Yes,' said Augusta. 'For once I agree with you, Agnes. It does make you feel old. I have really felt the burden of *my* years during the past few days. Still, never mind. By the time I'm ready to go, I suppose I'll be only too happy to hand over the reins.

Responsibility for other people is a huge burden, Agnes. You probably don't know what I'm talking about, but it's true. I have felt so conscious of that burden over the years, that I have probably been *too* careful, too sure that my

204

way was the only way. It's taken me a long time, and a great shock, to see the light. But better late than never, eh?'

Agnes gave Augusta a strange look. Did she know something? She was talking as if she was about to leave the planet. Agnes had never heard Augusta speak in these sorts of terms, and it was upsetting to her. For what she was about to do, she must concentrate on her hatred of the woman, and here she was softening up in front of her eyes.

Maybe she'd got the wind up? After all, just about everyone was gunning for Augusta now, placing themselves so that if something happened they would be in the best position to pick up the pieces.

Agnes looked at her watch. It was nine o'clock. If she was going to do it tonight, she would have to do it soon, but where was Laurens?'

As if in answer to her question there was the sound of the front door opening.

'Oh thank goodness for that. Wii...llll...iam!' she called out. 'Is that you?'

Laurens poked his head around the door.

'Someone want me?' he asked.

'Yes, William,' said Augusta, rising from the table. 'I need to talk to you, right away. Let's go to the library shall we. Excuse us, Agnes.'

Agnes flashed an agonized glance in Laurens direction, but he wasn't looking. She would have to wait until they'd finished.

Once in the library Augusta motioned Laurens to sit down. She herself stood, wringing her hands as if trying to work out where to start.

'First of all, William, I have to apologize. I know what I said the other night must have upset you greatly, and I had no cause to do that to you. You have been my support and my friend now for.... God knows how many years. You must consider me to be a first class bitch the way I've treated you. Well, now I acknowledge it, and I ask for your forgiveness, William.'

'Who knows, if I hadn't been such an impulsive and stupid young girl, I might have married you first off instead of Indigo, and saved us both a lot of heartache into the bargain. But you were so shy in those days, and I was so impatient. I always had to have my own way, didn't I, and the result was that I treated everyone else like dirt. I really am truly sorry, William. Do you accept my apology?'

Laurens looked stunned. He floundered with his mouth open, and finally said:

'Well! Put that way, how can I say no? Of course I do, Augusta.'

'Good. Then hear me out. I've had a lot of time to think about my life and my mistakes over the past few days, since they raised that empty coffin. The fact that it was empty punctured my pride; but I'm all right now. I'm sure Indigo was right when he said that I took everything from him, including his name. So I don't blame him for running off with the parlourmaid.'

Laurens waved madly at her as if to double-take. He couldn't believe what he'd just heard.

'Did you say 'empty' coffin? Was that coffin empty? I don't believe it!'

'Oh, that's right. You didn't know, did you? I'm sorry again. I was so distraught with the many and various implications that I didn't think to ease your mind over the matter. Only James and Frederick knew to this point in time.'

'Empty! I don't believe it,' Laurens repeated. He was staring into the middle distance like a man possessed. 'That....Bastard! Empty coffin, eh?'

'Yes, dear. He filled it with fifteen bricks and put a note in it for me should I dig 'him' up again. But in his footnote, he was right as usual. He knew I wouldn't. He'd already guessed that I couldn't face the scandal. I must have been *so* obvious.'

'Thirty three years. Thirty three blasted years, and every day I've thought about him, down in that coffin, struggling for breath, terrified....'

'I know dear. I know! Didn't we all. It turns out that he ran off with the under-parlourmaid, and god knows where they went, probably overseas.'

'So I'm free and clear,' Laurens muttered. 'There is no body!'

'That's right, William. There is no body. I'm sorry. I should have told you days ago. But it got me to thinking, William, and that was why I went to see our solicitors; which brings me to what I actually want to talk to you about.'

Laurens shook his head, and tried to hang on to what she was saying.

'About what? What else could there be?'

'I've decided to stop being such a worrier where it comes to money. I've always been what I thought was thrifty. I realize now that 'thrifty' can also mean tight. I've certainly been tight, William, and I've kept everyone on a short leash. Well, the news is that the family is a lot better off than even I thought it was, so I've decided to make everyone a bequest, now, before I die, so that you can all enjoy your lives again. I've instructed Mr. Game to make you out a cheque for $50,000 dear. I hope that will help to make up for my tardiness in the past.'

'Fifty.... My god, woman. Are you being serious?'

'Quite serious, William. Is that worth a hug?'

Laurens bounded out of his chair and danced her across the floor. Then he kissed her gently.

'I don't know what's come over you, Augusta, but I like it. I definitely like it.'

'I've also made provision for James, Agnes, Frederick, Mrs. Cherry and Joanne, in varying amounts, depending on their length of service, position in the family and so on.'

'Have you, by God! Oh God!' He stopped, and looked horror stricken. He'd just remembered Agnes, and the hypodermic.

'Yes; all I have to do is sign the cheques when they arrive here - is there something wrong, William?"

'No, not at all, Augusta. Sign the cheques; right! No - it's just that I've remembered something I had to attend to, and I forgot about it, that's all. I'll see to it later.'

'Now that we've sorted that out, I'm off to bed. Come up when you're ready.'

Laurens put his hand to his head, and said: 'Just wait a minute, will you Augusta. Give me two minutes before you go anywhere, I just have to check.'

He nipped out of the door, leaving Augusta looking bemused.

Outside in the main entrance hall, he scanned the area for Agnes, but she was nowhere to be seen. He went to the staircase, then through to the dining room – nothing. He had to stop her before it was too late.

Laurens went out into the kitchen to check, then half ran back. As he came out of the dining room again and reached the stairs, he saw the door of the romper room open and Agnes dash out, heading for the library. She was through the library door before he could get there, and the door slammed in his face.

III

Adam and Eugenia made their way back to the church, underground, and mounted the steps to the trapdoor. Presently they were back in the antechamber, and Eugenia followed him into his living area. Adam was quite high on the exercise, and couldn't stop talking. Eugenia pulled him onto the bed, and wrapped herself around him until he started tearing at her clothes, stripping her in his excitement. Eugenia laid herself open to him, and let him drive and thrust at will. She was more than obsessed with Pastor Adam.

Afterwards, his mood changed. He became silent and turned in on himself, and she realized it was time for her to leave. It was dark outside by this time, and she made her way across the cemetery, trying to keep her sense of direction by referring to the looming square of Valhalla in the gloom.

As she came along an aisle near the edge of the cemetery, she heard a noise, and stopped, thinking that someone might be following her. She looked behind, but could see nothing. As she turned back, a shape began to rise up in front of her, and as it rose she saw the face of her husband, Reginald, staring at her through the perspex. She froze as she looked at his face, and he stared back, unsmiling.

In her mind she heard his voice saying: 'Slut – Murderess - You will be damned in Hell forever!'

She felt her chest go tight, and experienced a shooting pain up her left arm.

'Slut – Husband killer! You die tonight!'

Eugenia slumped to her knees, and before she toppled forward onto her face, she saw the face of her husband slide grimly back into the ground.

IV

Back at the church, Adam sat staring into his fire. Outside, Richard Carstairs sat waiting for Brindy to re-appear. He had been waiting outside for two hours already, and was both cold and impatient. He had tried listening by the makeshift chimney, but found it strange that there was no noise at all. It was as if the building was empty. He slunk off and waited among the trees, but it was a long wait. When Eugenia left, he was taken by surprise. He couldn't make his mind up whether to follow her, or whether to wait for Brindy, whom he'd seen enter two hours before. Brindy won.

Eugenia had disappeared through the trees, and headed for the cemetery, Richard turned his attention to the door. Suddenly he made up his mind. He got up and made a mad charge at the door, kicked it open and charged inside.

'Brindy!' he yelled. 'Are you all right?'

Adam leapt to his feet and spun around just as Richard came crashing through his screens. In a moment they were grappling with each other on the floor, with Richard demanding to know where Brindy was.

'I know she's here, you bastard. I watched her come in. What have you done with her?'

Adam kicked and yelled in shock and surprise, and fought back. They both threw punches, and Adam got the worst of it.

'She left, she's not here,' he yelled desperately. 'Get off me you maniac!'

'She's still here, you bastard. I've been watching this place, and she couldn't have got past me without me seeing her.' Richard had his hands around Adam's throat.

'Get off me, she's gone. I don't know where she is,' yelled Adam, suddenly fearful for his life.

They rolled around the floor, and Richard landed half in the fire, scattering burning logs around the floor. Adam yelled as his bed started to burn, and small fires began to spring up all over. Within a minute the wooden floor had caught, and the two were still rolling around throwing punches. Suddenly Adam broke away and made a dash for the door, slamming it behind him.

Richard jumped to his feet and dashed in the same direction. The door was jammed. He kicked at it, pulled it, and rammed his shoulder against it, but it would not give. The church was beginning to fill up with smoke, and Richard began to gag. He pulled his shirt out and pressed it over his mouth, then ran back along the church looking for an alternative exit. The windows were set too high to get through without something to stand on, and there was nothing that he could see that was light enough to move on his own.

He picked up a hymn book and hurled it through one of the windows, and the moment it shattered a rush of fresh air blew through, fanning the flames even higher. He headed for the back of the church, and fell through a doorway into a small antechamber. The air was still relatively smokeless in there, and he looked around for another door. There was nothing. As he was about to dash out again, he caught sight of the trapdoor, and in a moment had it open and was heading down the stairs into the darkness.

Outside in the trees, Adam Cain watched as flames licked up through the roof, and burst the windows with its heat. No one could withstand that. He walked away, convinced that Dr. Richard Carstairs was already dead.

Chapter Thirteen

Agnes had been waiting in the romper room, eye at the crack in the door. She watched as Laurens came out, looking for her, but didn't realize that was what he wanted. She thought he was just getting out of her way so she could do the deed. When he disappeared in the direction of the main hall, she gritted her teeth, and concentrated on all the petty grievances she'd felt over the years. She had to build up her hatred of the woman to allow her to do this deed in good conscience.

When she judged the coast was clear, she slipped the cap off the needle, and held it in her hand like a dagger. Then raising her arm over her head, she thrust the door open and charged, racing across the passageway and flinging the library door open. She vaguely saw someone coming at her from the left, but didn't realize it was Laurens. She flew through the door and slammed it behind her, continuing her charge towards Augusta who was standing near a low table.

Augusta looked up, and saw this short, dumpy troglodyte coming at her, her arm up over her head. Always very quick in her movements, Augusta stepped aside, and Agnes caught her shins on the coffee table and flew head over heels onto the floor. When she sat up, she looked down to see the hypo sticking out of her own leg.

'What on earth are you thinking of, Agnes? Have you gone raving mad,' said Augusta, holding out a hand to help her up.

Agnes let out a wail of anguish, and then screamed.

'No, no, no, it's not fair!' she yelled, and bounded to her feet.

By this time Laurens had got in, and was standing by the doorway, a look of horror on his face. Agnes dashed by him and headed for her room, wailing all the way, and Augusta and he stood stunned, listening to her door slam shut in the distance. There was a sudden silence, and the two looked at each other.

'Is that what you meant when you said you just had to check? It seems I've misjudged you, William, all the way down the line!' Augusta said, grimly.

Without looking at him she stalked out of the library and headed for Agnes' room. Laurens followed, the sweat breaking out on his brow. Augusta didn't bother to knock, but just stormed in. Agnes was lying on the floor, twitching. The needle lay nearby. Augusta bent down and picked it up, being careful not to touch the needle.

'You'd better get rid of this, William. A jury might find it hard to understand where a middle-aged woman got a hypodermic filled with.... what is it filled with, William? Never mind. For old time's sake, and in the light of knowing now how much everyone hates me, I'll let you off the hook. Get rid of it!'

She handed the needle to William, who looked totally subdued.

'It's still mostly full, she can't have injected much. Will that make any difference?' she asked, looking at Agnes on the floor, who had now stopped twitching.

Laurens shook his head. He put the syringe down on the table, and went over to bend over Agnes. She was looking up at him with the fierce light of desperation in her eyes. She knew everything that was happening to her, but couldn't move a muscle. Her body seemed to have disappeared, because she couldn't feel any of it. He mind told her mouth to scream, but her brain was no longer in control of her body. Nothing responded.

'I'll deal with this,' said Laurens to Augusta. 'You'd better go to bed.'

'Very well, William. Do the very best you can,' said Augusta, quietly. 'It should never have come to this.'

She turned and left the room, looking more like an old woman now than she'd ever looked.

Laurens looked down at Agnes, and shook his head.

'I'm sorry old girl. It shouldn't have happened. I tried to find you to stop you, because Augusta has had a change of heart. She ordered the solicitor to make you out a cheque for $40,000, and another one for me. You would have been very comfortably off.'

The horror and the irony swept over Agnes in her strait-jacket of a body, but the only expression came out at her eyes. These disturbed Laurens so much that he looked away.

'We're going to have to look after you. Don't worry, I'll see you get the very best of whatever entertainment James can offer.'

He bent down and picked her up, placing her carefully into her coffin. She could see the lid looming above her, and Laurens face as he turned to say goodnight. Finding a small doorstop, he placed it on the edge of the coffin, and lowered the lid. That should give her enough air. She wouldn't be going anywhere from now on, anyway. Turning out the light, he left the room.

II

Edmund was working late that night. He had two of the three corpses of those who had died at Mrs. Bacon's funeral to do, and he was feeling rather stressed. In the distance he could hear the activity going on at Wally Kirk's engineering shop as they worked three shifts to assemble the improved, updated pop-ups. Where was Brindy Somers? She'd promised that once she'd attended to a bit of private business, she'd call in and get started on the make-overs. But there was no sign of her. At nine o'clock, Edmund phoned Janet Golightly, another girl from the beauty parlour, and offered her some part-time work. Janet jumped at the chance, and was there by 9.20pm.

Just before ten, an urchin from the town stuck his head in the door and said:

'Mister! There's a body in the cemetery!'

Thinking it was the lad's idea of a joke, Edmund replied, drolly, 'I'm sure there are hundreds of bodies in the cemetery, lad. That's what cemeteries are for.'

'No, really Mister. I just saw it. A woman, lyin' on her face on the ground. I think she's dead!'

Edmund followed the boy to the spot by Reginald's pop-up, and found Eugenia lying there on her face, well and truly extinct. As he stood there, Reginald's pop-up slid up two feet out of the ground, just high enough for Reg's head to be showing. The muscles in the face had shrunk somewhat, and the mouth had been drawn into a definite grin. Reginald appeared to be looking at his dead wife in glee. Then it slid back into the ground. Edmund looked puzzled. There must be some fault with that, he'd have to get Werner to have a look at it.

He returned to the parlour and called out the local constable, directing him over the phone to where he'd find the body. Then he gave the lad $5 for his trouble, and told him to push off. The body was picked up and delivered to the hospital morgue for examination, though Constable Porter couldn't raise Dr. Carstairs, so he got onto Dr. Laurens over at the Great Hall, and got him to call in.

Meanwhile, Dr. Carstairs was standing in a tunnel, under the old church, watching the flooring and burning embers block the way he had escaped. The tunnel was starting to get smoky too, so by the dim light of the fire behind him Richard set off along the tunnel, trying to find out where it led. After a hundred yards the tunnel branched, and Richard stood trying to see in the deepening gloom which way to go. He decided to keep going ahead, though the light was barely enough to see his hand in front of his face. He bumped into walls and fell over a few times where there was rubble on the floor, but kept pushing on with caterpillar slowness. After what seemed like forever, the tunnel branched again, into three this time. It was obviously a major drive cutting across the main tunnel, so Richard decided to take the right hand fork.

This was not a long tunnel. It may have been once, but a major rock fall had closed it off thirty yards along. He tried to find a way around it, feeling with his hands, but it seemed like a dead end. Climbing up the rock fall on the right hand side, he felt up above him for the roof. His hand came to rest on a wooden step. There was no doubt about it, he could feel the bottom of a doorway, though it was so black down there that he couldn't see a thing. He scrabbled around, trying to get a foothold so he could climb higher, and then he felt a door set behind the step. If he could only pull himself high enough, he could try it.

After two or three minutes of scrabbling around without success, he hoisted himself onto the step itself, and stopped to get his strength back. At that moment he heard a noise, and the door suddenly flew open, so suddenly that he was caught unprepared and he fell through the doorway, into the light.

'Gotcha!' said Joanne Destry.

III

Joanne had left the table saying she felt like an early night, though that was just a blind. She had the South Wing on the brain, and wanted to go back there at night, thinking that she might be able to lie in wait for whoever it was that was haunting the place. Twice now she had heard another presence, and yet discreet enquiries had assured her that the Wing had been locked up for years, and that no one went there anymore. There was a mystery in that itself.

Finding her little room, she had left the door ajar so as to be able to hear any disturbance, and had sat back at the desk. The maps she'd already seen, or all of them that interested her, anyway. She pulled further documents out of the pigeon holes, and moodily glanced through them. More bills, statements, and the odd note to a servant:

> *'Annie,*
>
> *Please be sure to order gammon, not bacon, and tell Mr. Styles that it must be properly smoked this time. Also, stock up on claret as we are running low.*
> *Eliza.'*

Sitting back, Joanne tried to imagine what Eliza Coverleigh had been like. She saw her as a short, bossy woman, with some of the asperity of her daughter, Augusta. She imagined that she ran the house with an iron fist, keeping tabs on everybody and everything. She wondered if she had known what happened to her brother, Randolph? No one would ever know, now.

As she sat back, she looked down and noticed two drawers in the left hand side of the desk. Funny that she hadn't noticed them before. Sliding one open she found pens, rubbers, pencils, an old packet of powdered ink, but no papers. In the second drawer there appeared to be nothing. She pulled it out a little further, and saw at the very back of the drawer a pile of letters, tied together with a silk ribbon. Her heart jumped into her mouth. She pulled them out of the drawer, and with shaking hands untied the ribbon.

Going through the envelopes there were letters here to Eliza, Richard Branwood, Sebastian and even Miles Coverleigh. Halfway down the pile there was a letter addressed to Margaret Chapland. Joanne nearly dropped it in her excitement. She looked for a postmark, but it had obviously never been sent. The envelope was blank. Inside there was just one sheet of paper.

June 26, 1928
Dearest Margt.

I see from the tone of yr. last letter that you have resigned yourself to spinsterhood, as y. say ye have not heard from me. I did indeed write, but the letter must have been intercept'd by yr. father, who has no love for anything Coverleigh. I stress again my love to you, and determination to wed, once obstacles have been removed by interested parties.

You are my little mare, my spanking pony, and I wd. not conceive of a life without you at my side. We will overcome, my love, and you shall keep that little love child yet.

Randolph.

Joanne jumped out of her seat, and bobbed up and down on the spot in her excitement. Proof – proof that there had been a child, at least. She put the letter in her pocket, and went back to the pile, looking for more. There was one to Eliza, from someone called Arnold Cobb, dated the same year.

August 15, 1928
  Mrs. Eliza Branwood
  (In Confidence).

The enquiries you requested have been completed, with no further indications than previously reported. The engineer has dealt with the collapsed shaft, and it should trouble you no further. The gardener Bursted has suggested a rock garden to decorate and camouflage the area, and I suggest you take his advice.

All mines and drives are now sealed to present knowledge, with access restricted to Sth. Wing. Suggest that door be boarded or bricked to give you future peace of mind. In the absence of proof, court action highly unlikely to proceed even if the worst happens, viz. the return of R.....
. Dr. Horton has confirmed diagnosis of approaching GPI, so safe to claim succession by default. Minimum publicity advised. I will be in touch as to my fee.

Yrs. Faithfully,
Arnold Cobb
Solicitor.

It was at this point that Joanne heard the footsteps. She froze in her seat, and listened, but could not tell where they were coming from. She went to the door, and peered out. They seemed to be coming from a passageway further over in the building, not the one closest to her.

She slipped out of the door, and tip-toed her way along the passage to the main passageway cutting across, and coming from the ballroom. It was definitely not there, she could see to both ends of the passage and there was no one. The footsteps got further away, heading south, and she was sure they came from a passage along the rear of the Wing.

Cutting back and into the ballroom, she looked for another exit. Sure enough, there was another passageway running off from behind a small room that had been used for hats and cloaks, thus obscuring the beginning of the passage from the ballroom. She began to run, chasing these footsteps now, until she heard a door slam ahead of her somewhere. Then the footsteps stopped. She was lost. There must have been twelve rooms in that section, and she had no idea which one the intruder had entered.

She began to go along the passageway, trying each door, looking around the room, then trying the next. She did this three times, making sure she'd checked every room, and then she sat down in the last room and left the door open, thinking that whoever it was would have to come back sooner or later, and would walk past that door.

She had armed herself with a snooker cue in the meantime, that she had found in what had once been a billiards room. The table was gone, but the heavy indents from the feet were still there in the carpet, and the cue was standing against a far wall. Now in the end room, she settled down to wait. It was almost an hour before she heard anything further. When she did it was like a scraping noise from out in the passageway. She walked cautiously out to track it down, and where the passage took a left turn at the end, she walked along to find a door she hadn't noticed before. It was recessed well back into the wall, so you couldn't see it unless you were almost on top of it.

She heard more scrabbling, and it seemed to be coming from the other side of the door. Her heart in her mouth, she reached for the handle, turned it and pulled.

No one was more surprised than she when Dr. Richard Carstairs fell into the passage, looking as if he'd been rolling in mud.

'Gotcha!' she said.

'Thank god for you,' he replied.

Chapter Fourteen

Brindy Somers lay in the coffin, terrified, the silence closing in around her like cotton wool in her ears. There was no light at all, and only the fact that a hole had been cut out of the lid just above her face stopped her going crazy on the spot. The other coffin was sitting about two inches above the hole, so she could breath without any problem, but the air was rank with the smell of death and decay. She tried forcing the lid, but it didn't give a millimeter. She was not only locked in, but the weight of the other coffin on top of her would have stopped her getting out.

From time to time she thought she heard sounds, very slight sounds, and then a scurrying sound made her think of rats. She was suddenly petrified. The claustrophobia of being enclosed like this was bad enough, without having to deal with her fear of rats. Then she realized she was quite safe from them, because the other coffin was on top, shielding her face.

The tears started rolling down her cheeks, making her hair and the pillow wet, but she couldn't help it. She made little sound as she cried, because the tears were involuntary. Brindy was usually pretty tough, and she wasn't going to give in to this.

What an animal that Pastor had turned out to be! And that woman, old Mrs. Barry! She was a slut of the first water, despite her age. She was fawning over Adam like a lovesick teenager.

Incredible how people got carried away with sex! Richard was the same – totally obsessed with her body. Brindy looked on all things as merely functions, bodily functions, mental functions, emotional functions. She believed in control, and never let herself get so far removed that she couldn't snap back and take control of a situation. It wasn't that she didn't like sex, she did; but she wasn't prepared to subjugate her life to it. There were other things just as appealing in her eyes.

Life itself was enough. She had discovered that when first being diagnosed with a tumour. All of a sudden, everything was sweet, the breeze, the trees rustling and swaying in the evenings, a hot bath, eating cherries and spitting out the pips, she could name a million things that she enjoyed doing, but dying wasn't one of them.

She didn't place a great deal of stock in relationships. She'd had a few, and they'd all ended in the same way. Either the partner had tried to take over her life, or she'd become the victim of jealousy, precluded from seeing her own friends, and made to conform to a pattern acceptable to the partner. She found that people could never accept you for what you were, they had to choke you all the time, try to change you. That last always seemed ludicrous to her because, if they'd been drawn to the qualities she'd displayed as a single person, to change those qualities, or suppress them would be to deny those things which caused the attraction in the first place. Thus, once she found these patterns repeating she could mercilessly end the relationship, with no thought of relenting or going back to it. To her, this was survival at its most basic. She was determined to survive intact.

She lay with her arms pinned at her sides, totally unable to move in the confines of this terrible box. Coffins weren't built with the idea of spaciousness; indeed, they were designed to afford as little space as possible, to house an inanimate shell, which had ceased to need room to move. But she, Brindy, was not an inanimate shell. She was alive and breathing and aware, and to put her into a coffin was an exquisite torture, thought up by a madman with a power complex.

What made it worse, she thought, was that some of her last moments of life were being squandered in the manner of the dead, when death was all, she had been told, that she had left to look forward to. So this was her future! This was what it was going to be like. That thought was enough in itself to make her demented, to cause her to froth at the mouth and injure herself, to cause her to want to fall into death's black, bottomless pit of unknowingness.

She must have lost consciousness for a while, because she remembered coming to with a start, thinking that she must have heard some movement. Then she did hear a movement! Someone was moving stealthily around inside this room. She heard a definite tread, and then she screamed, and began to sob uncontrollably, unable to take this final shredding of her nerves and her self-respect.

There was a scraping, and then she realized that the coffin on top was being lifted off her and dumped on the ground. Oh, thank god, Adam must have had second thoughts.

'Is that you Adam,' she sobbed, 'Oh get me out of here. This is terrible, terrible...' and she went off into another wave of uncontrolled sobbing.

She felt rather than heard the shifting of the bolt that held the coffin lid down, and she waited for the lid to be raised. But it wasn't. She heard very clearly the slab move back into place, as if someone had just left. She pushed, and the lid came up easily, and the cold night air touched her body, making her realize how much she had sweated in that box. She lay for a minute, trying to summon up enough strength to get up, to physically drag herself out of her prison, and she found that it took almost every ounce of strength she had. She stood beside the box, shaking, looking at the different piles of coffins in the room, and then she turned and saw that there was a door, and it was standing ajar, bidding her fly through it to freedom. She staggered to the door and out, and she was standing in the cemetery, outside a family vault of black marble, and inscribed in gold lettering over the arch was the name – 'Varley'.

Turning, she saw a glow in the distance, and realized that she was looking at the last smouldering moments of the little church she had visited earlier that night. There was a fire engine and firemen playing water on the walls, and flames leaping up from inside still, showing brightly against the sky where there had once been a roof. Brindy staggered off through the headstones, trying to put as much space as she could between her and that church.

II

James came striding into the Great Hall, unhappy that he'd been dragged out of bed by a late call from Laurens. The doctor had just returned from the hospital, where he'd certified Eugenia Barry dead of a heart attack. The only strange thing he could see about the case was the look of absolute horror that had been frozen onto her features at the moment of death. Other than that, he saw no point in proceeding to an autopsy. She was almost sixty after all, and she *had* just suffered the trauma of losing her husband to a particularly nasty sort of accidental death. He signed the death certificate, and a release form for the body to be picked up by Pepper's funerals. There was nothing else he could do.

All the time he had been away, Laurens mind had been grappling with the problem of Agnes. Released from one threat, that of Indigo's recent resurrection, he was faced now with another threat, that of the attempted murder of Augusta; or supplying Agnes with the wherewithal, and now the paralysis of Agnes. He could have just shut the coffin lid on her without inserting a spacer, he realized, and the attempted murder of one could have been converted into the murder of another. Life was full of choices!

Somehow he just couldn't bring himself to do it. He was prepared to give it a few hours to see if there were any positive signs – she had, after all, only injected a tiny amount into her leg, and her body might just shake it off – but failing that, he was going to have to make a decision. Was it Agnes for the high jump, or Agnes for a prolonged life support system? He knew which decision would have been easiest, but he was constrained to wait.

By the time he got back from the hospital he thought that he'd better enlist family support, and phoned James in the North Wing who had just got into bed. Reluctantly James agreed to come down, and when he saw the shape Agnes was in, he was glad that he had.

'How did this happen? Is she going to recover,' said James, aware that he still had a pact with Agnes concerning the demise of Augusta.

'She tried to kill Augusta,' said Laurens, avoiding any mention of his part in the episode.

'She was going to stick her with some poison in a syringe, but fell over and stuck herself instead. She's fully paralyzed, and it's doubtful whether or not she'll recover. She's still fully conscious, that's the problem. She could get some control back, anything could happen, but if not she needs to be kept somewhere we can keep an eye on her. She has certain information that, in the wrong hands, if you know what I mean?'

James olive complexion turned a sickly green. So she'd told Laurens. The stupid bitch! He should have known better than to think she could keep her mouth shut.

Laurens watched him closely, and saw the reaction. So he *was* right! James had involved himself with her in a plot to get rid of Augusta. God, they were all in it.

'I think I can depend on your discretion, James,' said Laurens.

'You can depend on me, that goes without saying,' said James. 'And I'm sure that I can depend on you, too.'

'Oh, indubitably James. We'll see this through together. By the way, I don't want to put your hopes up unnecessarily, but Augusta informed me tonight, before this unfortunate event occurred, that you were to receive a cheque next week for a considerable sum of money. Something in the region of $50,000.'

James flinched.

'Is that right? Well, thank you for that information, doctor, I shall keep it under my hat. Let's just hope that Augusta hasn't changed her mind due to Agnes's bad timing.'

'Bad timing indeed,' breathed Laurens.

'I suggest that as an interim measure we install Agnes in the highest vault of 'HEAVEN', the seventh level. She will have plenty of time to think up there, and will only be interrupted by Gabriel's incessant harping. If she does then come around, so to speak, we may hope that her mind has not become too unhinged.'

'What if it has?' said the doctor, meaningfully.

'Well, a quick visit to the embalming lab might be called for. But I'm sure that, given a reasonable warning, we can prevail upon her not to progress on to the next level. Life is good,' James smiled.

'Death is better,' grinned Laurens, parodying the slogan of the funeral parlour.

III

All this time Agnes had been staring fixedly at the ceiling since they had opened the coffin lid. Her mind was screaming at them: 'Do something, get me an antidote or something, you can't leave me like this!'

She lay there listening to their conversation, reading between the lines, understanding the knife-edge she was on. It was so unfair. They'd both wanted Augusta dead, and now she was paying for it, and they were getting off scot free. Neither of them had wanted to do the deed, they were quite happy to use her, and now here she lay, helpless, subject to their arbitrary decisions, and unable to defend herself. If she could have cried, she would, but she didn't even have any control over that any more.

Why hadn't she just leaned over at the tea table and casually injected the thing into Augusta's arm while she was still seated. It would have been so easy, and all over in minutes. Then she would have been all right, and Augusta would have been in a coffin somewhere. That woman always came up smiling. It enraged Agnes, who had spent a lifetime watching Augusta come out of bad deals as if she had won the lottery. Fortune always smiled on her while she, Agnes, had always had the rough end of the stick. Now it had happened again.

She watched the ceiling start moving above her as the coffin was loaded onto a trolley and wheeled out of her beloved room. She was even going to lose her view. Out in the night, it wasn't long before she was being wheeled in under the giant horns of Valhalla, the doors creaking open to receive her. She could hear the cacophony of 'HELL' as she was drawn in, and the ticking of the metronome as she travelled past 'PURGATORY'. Then she was on an elevator and rising towards a white ceiling, the coffin being off-loaded onto a conveyor, and then travelling to her final resting place, level 7, row 10, coffin 7. It was an out of the way position, unlikely to be frequented by visitors. That was the beauty of the 'HEAVEN' clients, James thought. Once safely relocated in their new homes, relatives of heavenly cadavers rarely visited them ever again. Not like in 'HELL' where there were distractions for the living as well as for the dead.

Agnes found herself staring at her own body, in a full-length mirror suspended from the ceiling. She watched as she was stripped, washed, redressed in a mortuary gown, allowing for easy access, and catheterized, the tube running into a container by the coffin. She was lain on a rubber sheet, then tubes inserted through her nose and down into her throat to allow her to be drip-fed. She felt none of this. But she was humiliated by the process, and began to wish that maybe they should have finished her off, rather than subject her to these indignities. She felt exposed to the common gaze, to any Tom, Dick or Harry who happened to be passing. It was an excruciating image, and one she was going to be forced to stare at permanently.

IV

Joanne stepped back, as Richard Carstairs lay on the floor, exhausted.

'So you're the ghostly visitor? I thought it would have been someone from the Great Hall,' said Joanne.

'I don't know what you're talking about,' said Richard, 'but babble on if it makes you feel better.' He leant back on his elbows, and took a few deep breaths.

'Didn't you walk through here about an hour ago? I heard the footsteps, but by the time I got here, they'd gone.'

'Not me! I've just come one way, from the old church by the cemetery. And that should be just about burnt to the ground by now. It was pretty well blazing when I left."

'What, the old Wesleyan Chapel?'

'That's right; and when I get hold of that Pastor Adam Cain, I'm going to have him for attempted murder, not to mention kidnapping.'

Richard explained how he went looking for Brindy Somers, saw her enter the church but not come out, and how he and Cain had fought. Then the fire, and how he had been locked in the building while Adam Cain escaped.

'You have had an eventful night, haven't you? Come on! I'll take you back to the Great Hall, and you can clean yourself up. I don't know if you know what you look like, but if you walk the streets like that, you'll be arrested.'

'Thanks,' he said, getting to his feet. But after that, I have to go and look for Brindy. I know he's got her hidden somewhere, and I wouldn't be surprised if she's down one of those tunnels. There are quite a few that go off at right angles.'

'I'd like to go down there myself,' said Joanne as they walked through the ballroom. 'I've got a personal interest in this old place, and I'm trying to get at the bottom of a mystery. I feel that I'm just getting to the edge of something at last, but it's still eluding me.'

Richard didn't ask, he was too busy with his own thoughts about Brindy.

'Well, at least he can't go back to the old church now,' he said. 'Which means he has nowhere to go. I'll check Brindy's place, in case he's holed up there, and then some of his other sycophants. Anyway, I just hope Brindy's all right. As long as she's not damaged.'

Joanne thought that was a strange turn of phrase to use about one's girlfriend. Not damaged? Unhurt would have been more appropriate.

Back in the Great Hall, Joanne found Richard a change of clothing, courtesy of Dr. Laurens. He cleaned himself up and then sat down to a hot drink to take the chill off.

'You haven't explained why you were down that end tonight,' he said, as Joanne sat opposite him. 'I thought the South wing was deserted these days. It's been closed up for years.'

'So it has,' said Joanne, 'but I had a reason. Can you keep a secret?'

'Do you mean, *will* I keep a secret? I don't see why not.'

'Okay. It's just that my position here is very tenuous, I wouldn't like to lose it just now.'

'I wouldn't dream of endangering your job.'

Richard looked at her speculatively. What dread secret could an attractive red-headed woman have? She seemed so homely.

'I'm interested in what happened to Randolph Coverleigh, back in 1928. You see he had an affair with my great grandmother, and I believe that I am descended from the result of that affair. I just can't prove it.'

'I see,' said Richard. 'So if that could be proved, you would become eligible to share in the family fortune. You might even inherit part of the estate once Augusta goes. How do you know he had this affair?'

'It was pretty well open knowledge. Her father disapproved, and tried to break them up. Then Randolph completely disappeared. He was never found. There was a daft story that he'd eloped with Margaret Chapland's horse – you know, there were allegations of bestiality in the family. But neither horse nor rider ever turned up again. But...' and here Joanne's eyes shone. 'There was always the story that he left Margaret 'with child', though there's never been any way of confirming that – until tonight! Look at this.'

She pulled out the letter that she'd pocketed from Randolph to Margaret. Richard read it, and handed it back.

'That's pretty convincing. Where did you find that?'

'In a drawer in a desk, in the South Wing tonight. I'm hanging on to it.'

'I don't blame you. Was there anything else?' Richard said, interested at last.

'I haven't had time to read them all. But I'll get around to it over the next few days. There should be some interesting reading there.'

'You'll have to let me know how you get on,' said Richard.

Joanne sat musing for a while after he had left. If *he* hadn't been the footsteps she'd heard, then who else could it be?

Chapter Fifteen

It was going to be a big day for Edmund. Three pop-up funerals to be completed in a row. Those who had died at Mrs. Bacon's funeral were now ready for interment themselves. The television stations were expected to be there, so this had to be a statement, a counter to all the advertising that Valhalla had been indulging in over the past few days.

As a result, Edmund had gone into a huddle with Werner over what the possibilities were, and Werner, not to be outdone, had designed an extravaganza fit for the viewers. There was a last minute rush to get everything in place before the cameras arrived, and a surprise appearance to be announced later.

Out in the cemetery, the square pods were waiting in line with Reginald Barry's pop-up. This was going to be a spectacle worth seeing. For the first time the perspex coffins were going to be set in place in front of the mourners. This meant that everything must go off like clockwork, no last minute technical problems.

Werner stood by the sidelines, with a creditable array of electronics at his disposal. He had a multiple controller, radio controlled, which wouldn't have looked out of place in an electronics exhibition. But he himself was partly hidden by an ancient headstone, as he didn't want to detract from the spectacle.

Nearby was Jonathon Pepper, the nervous figurehead, not quite comfortable with the new way of doing things, and happy to hand over the position of master of ceremonies to Edmund. Twenty yards from Edmund, and taking a great interest in proceedings, was James Coverleigh, looking like a South American drug dealer, who had popped over to see what all the fuss was about.

When the mourners filed out of the chapel, a small converted truck, painted black, pulled out from the back of the chapel and drove around to the gravesites. From a rail along the back of the vehicle dangled three perspex coffins. The headstones were already in place, the contents of each coffin hidden by a black curtain drawn around the four sides. Pulling up beside each pod in turn, a coffin was slipped off the rail and dropped into place, each operation taking about twenty seconds. Within three minutes the truck pulled away, leaving the three tower-like coffins standing, draped in black, and looking menacing under a darkening sky.

Edmund stepped up to a microphone, and began his piece.

'Ladies and gentlemen,

You are here today to pay tribute to these brave pioneers, the first casualties of the new wave of high-tech in the funeral industry. They are the first, but will not be the last, to voluntarily give up their lives in order that they may fuel the pursuit of excellence in many a refurbishing industry. These are they who are building between them a truly brave new world. We salute them, and in their honour we make available to them, and to their future descendants, the very latest in the art of Death History – Themselves!'

At this, the curtains around the coffins were lowered to the ground, revealing the three unfortunate victims of Mrs. Bacon. They were all dressed in contemporary clothes, looking natural and fresh, each make-over done exceptionally well by Janet Golightly the night before. The crowd began to clap politely, when, to their surprise, the corpses straightened slightly and began to applaud the crowd. This made the crowd applaud even more, and suddenly they were cheering, and the cameramen were frantically panning in, out and along as the cadavers clapped.

In the meantime, the church choir had taken up their position in front of the three coffins, and a five-man band stood by to provide the backing. Unseen by most, a small motorized trolley was heading out from the side of the chapel. Edmund put his hands in the air, and the cameras focussed on him.

'People...people,' he called, looking for silence. 'I'm proud today, to present to you – by special request – the second public appearance of...'

The motorized trolley had halted in front of the choir, a slip cloth was pulled away, revealing a coffin on the trolley. The lid sprang open and who should pop up, baton in hand, but....

'...Mrs. Bacon!' The mourners roared.

Mrs. Bacon rapped twice on the side of her coffin, and began to conduct the choir in 'Onward Christian Soldiers'. The cameramen were beside themselves, maneuvering their cameras around to take in the scene of the choir, the dead conductor, and the three upright corpses. Within half a minute, there was a general nudging through the crowd – the cadavers were waving their hands in time to the music. It was

Edmund's moment of glory. A gravesite service with choir, three cadavers, and a dead music teacher!

Werner in the background was in his element. At the end of the hymn, Mrs. Bacon rapped twice again, and electronically the sound of the notes from 'Close Encounters of the Third Kind' came from the speakers. As they did so, the coffins in turn dipped into the ground, and came up again. Each coffin responded to a different note, so the effect was quite spectacular. They began diving and shooting in sequence as the music was repeated, the coffins bobbing up and down like the pistons in a car.

The mourners went wild, jumping up and down in time to the coffins, and the cameramen dashed to new vantage points yet again. James Coverleigh shook his head and turned away. He had seen all he wanted to see, and headed back to Valhalla. He'd have to talk to the engineers again.

The six o'clock news was a major triumph. The clips went national, and within a few hours they had been picked up by CNN and were being flashed onto American screens. Edmund was suddenly world famous. He had to take the phone off the hook, because there were over 2,000 logged calls in an hour and a half, and he went home, directing Jonathon that he wasn't to be disturbed for 24 hours.

II

Augusta spent the morning staring out of the window at Valhalla. She could see the activity going on over the other side, but she was too distracted to take any interest. She had called in to Agnes' room that morning, to find she'd gone. She went in search of Laurens, and asked what had been done with her.

'Don't worry, Augusta, I've arranged to have her looked after. She's up in 'HEAVEN' on a drip, we're just waiting to see if there's any improvement.'

'What do you think are her chances,' said Augusta, subdued.

'I really have no idea. She's not going to die, if that's what you mean. But she might as well if she doesn't recover some feeling shortly.'

Augusta was silent for a moment.

'I know you had something to do with this, William. She didn't get that syringe on her own. But in the light of what I've been thinking lately, I'm not going to push you on it. But I do feel desperately sorry for Agnes. I want you to do everything possible to get her back to normal, no expense spared.'

Laurens looked at her, and held out his hand.

'I've been a bloody fool, Augusta. You're one in a million. You make me feel small.'

'No, William. Don't! I blame myself entirely. I have a lifetime to repent, you only have a final frustration to put behind you. The same with Agnes, the poor, silly, misguided woman. You must help her, William.'

'I know,' he said.

After lunch, Augusta set out for Valhalla, and entered unannounced. James guided her to the visitor's lift at the 'HEAVEN' end, and told her which way to go. She ascended to the seventh level, and walked along the walkway, looking for Agnes. When she got to row 10, she walked slowly along until she came to coffin 7, and burst into tears.

Agnes was lying motionless with an expressionless look on her face. Augusta took out a handkerchief and wiped her face, and put her arms around her to hug her.

'I'm so sorry, Agnes. I'm so, so sorry. I know what you tried to do last night, and I forgive you for that. God, how you must hate me! I've been very wrong, cousin, very very wrong. If you can find it in your heart I want you to forgive me. I intend to pursue every opportunity to make you well again, and I'll spare no expense. Things are going to change, Agnes. I promise! We'll make you well again, and we'll be friends, Agnes. We'll be equals. I promise I'll never try to make you feel like a second-rate citizen again. You'll have your own money, and your own car. I want you to fight this thing for me, fight it, Agnes.'

Agnes saw and heard but could not feel Augusta's hug. She couldn't believe what she was hearing. What a fool she'd been. What fools they'd all been. If she could only go back twenty-four hours, but it was too, too late. She was paralyzed, and she would probably die. Nothing Augusta could do would help her now. Two tiny tears squeezed out from the corners of her eyes, and rolled down her cheeks.

III

Brindy Somers had staggered home that night, saturated with sweat and freezing in the night air. When she got to her little flat she almost fell in through the door, her legs were so weak from her ordeal. She considered phoning the local constable, but couldn't face being up all night, answering questions and filling out a statement. She just wanted to sleep,

She ran a bath for herself and went around locking all the doors and windows in case Adam was prowling around, though she was unsure if he knew where she lived. She lay in the bath, luxuriating in the heat, and getting the smell of decaying flesh out of her skin and hair. She would have to change her occupation. Working with cadavers was beginning to spill out into her life at large. All she seemed involved in lately was death.

She suddenly found herself crying uncontrollably. The thought of being confined forever in a box had settled deep into her mind, and she made a mental note that she would put in her will an instruction that she be cremated. Far better that she burn, than spend eternity confined like that. She knew it was irrational, that if she were dead she would know nothing about it, but those few hours had been so horrifying that she would never feel comfortable again with the idea of burial. She got out of the bath and towelled herself dry, throwing on some pyjamas and putting out the light, ready for bed.

She had no sooner pulled the covers over her than she heard movements outside her window. She froze. 'Oh God, not Adam!' She lay there in terror, listening for the slightest sound, but all she could hear was the rustling of the trees outside her window. It was some time before she managed to drop off to sleep.

Adam meanwhile, had nowhere to go. He sat on a headstone in the cemetery watching as the fire engine arrived, and the futile battling of the flames. But it was obvious that nothing would be saved. He cursed Richard Carstairs roundly, and wondered if they would find his body in the embers. There wouldn't be much left of him, and if they asked he would say that he was out taking the air when it happened, and that by the time he got back, the place was a blazing ruin. If they mentioned a body, he'd say it must have been an intruder, or a member of his congregation looking for guidance. Until the doctor was found to be missing, it was unlikely that they'd be able to identify the body.

Some movement on the other side of the cemetery attracted his attention, and he ran, crouching toward the figures, but hidden by the headstones. He didn't want to be seen just now. As he got closer he saw the body of a woman lying face down, and the local constable taking photographs with a flash. When Porter rolled her over, Adam recognized the body as that of Eugenia, his faithful slave. She was more than obviously dead.

He withdrew into the middle of the cemetery where the darkness was all enveloping, sat on a slab and cursed. So much for sixty thousand dollars! That could have bought his ticket out of here. The situation was getting out of hand. Two bodies, and both connected to him in some way. If Brindy was released, and told the authorities her story, he would be going to gaol for a long time. He began to perspire, despite the cold, and his hands began to shake. He knew what he had to do. There was no question now, he'd have to make sure that Brindy never got the opportunity to tell anyone.

He thought of her, trapped in that coffin. It seemed a good idea at the time, and he had been carried away by the thought that he could make her come to heel if he showed her he meant business. She had obsessed him with her body, and he couldn't stand the thought that she had no feeling for him whatsoever. No woman had ever said that to him before. They had always fought to be first into his bed. It was a new experience for him.

He got up and made his way to a large mausoleum in the middle of the cemetery, its dark, forbidding shape appearing in relief against the night sky. He could just make out the name 'Varley' above the door, and walked in closer to see if there was any way he could get in. The tunnel was closed off now by the collapsing church, so he'd have to find another way.

As he came in close, he saw that one of the doors was ajar. He stopped, with a sudden feeling of apprehension. Those doors had been locked before, and he hadn't touched them! He cautiously poked his head inside, listening.

'Brindy! Hey, Brindy! It was just a joke. I'm coming to let you out,' he whispered. He sidled into the dark chamber, and walked over to where he had left one coffin on top of another. It was all right, they were still in place! He breathed a sigh of relief, and began to manhandle the top coffin onto the ground.

'Sorry about this, Brindy. But it seems you've become a bit of a liability. I'm going to have to get rid you.'

There was a creak from behind, and he sprang around, defensively, just in time to see the door close behind him. There was the sound of a bolt sliding into place, then nothing. He ran to the door and tried it – locked. The doors were big and solid, the hinges on the outside. There was no way he'd get through them. He made his way around to where the moveable marble slab had given him access from the tunnel, but that was firmly set in place, and there was no mechanism inside the vault to open it.

'Damn and blast it. Who the bloody hell is playing games,' he exploded, and then remembered Brindy in her coffin.

'Well, it's not going to help you any, Brindy. Once you're dead I'll just put you into another coffin with an old corpse. They'll never find you.'

There was no answer, and the silence made him panic.

'Did you hear what I said, Brindy?'

He felt his way back to the coffins, and finally found hers, down on the ground. Then he felt around for where her face should be. Nothing! The hole was there, but no face. Brindy had gone.

The temperature seemed to drop five degrees, and Adam shivered as he realized that he'd been caught in a trap.

Chapter Sixteen

Eugenia Barry was a problem! There were no living relatives thank goodness, thought Edmund, or he might have to go back to a standard burial for her. The problem was her face. No matter how much he pummelled and kneaded, pinched the flesh between finger and thumb, or smoothed and patted, that look of absolute horror and terror continued to reassert itself on her features. It was as if her muscles had set at the moment of death, and no amount of reshaping was going to relax them. She was embalmed with the horror of everlasting hell on her features, and Edmund didn't want a group of mourners seeing that. So he arranged for her to be slipped into the ground unobtrusively, without any fanfare.

Werner came over and helped with the arrangements. The hole had been dug, opposite Reginald's plot so that the two could be together. It just remained to slot the coffin into position, and drive it down.

'That reminds me, Werner. There seems to be something wrong with the drive mechanism for Reginald's pop-up, because the coffin pops-up at the most inconvenient times.'

'It is probably zuh short circuit. If it is wet, zen maybe it makes zuh contact and zoom! Ve vill fix him tomorrow!'

They brought Eugenia out on the back of the truck and dropped her into the slot. She stood there, staring at some phantom in the distance, facing Reginald's gravesite. Edmund put the key in the lock and she slid noiselessly into the ground. He pulled the key out and they went to walk away. As they did they heard a whirr, and turned back. Reginald's pop-up had slid up a foot, just enough for his eyes to be seen staring across at his wife's headstone.

'See what I mean. It's popped up again. You're going to have to de-activate it.'

Before Werner could reply, Eugenia's coffin popped up two feet, and Reginald's another foot, so they were staring at each other across a space of about three feet. There was a devilish grin on Reginald's face, and the fixed look of horror on Eugenia's. They then both slid into the ground. Werner looked at Edmund, then went over and with a pair of wire cutters, disconnected both pop-ups from the power line.

He walked back, grinning. 'Let's see zem beat zat!'

As if in answer to his jibe, Reginald's coffin slid silently up three feet, and Eugenia's a foot. They stared at one another for a minute, then sank bank into the ground together. Werner shook his head.

'Zat is impossible,' he said. 'Vucking impossible!'

'As you said, fucking impossible,' echoed Edmund, shaking his head.

They stood there for another two minutes, watching intently. When nothing further happened they walked away, leaving Reginald and Eugenia to their eternal rest.

II

Brindy Somers slept in until ten fifteen, and awoke feeling as if she had just come out of a bad dream. Then the events of the previous evening started coming back to her, and she jumped out of bed to check all the doors and windows, to see if any had been tampered with. Everything seemed to be in place, much to her relief. She thought about Adam Cain, and wondered where he had gone now that the church lay in ruins. Was he lying in wait for her somewhere, getting ready to drag her off, back to that vault, and imprison her in that coffin – or worse. She shuddered, and threw her clothes on, not knowing what course of action to take. She could go to the police, but that would involve her in all sorts of unpleasantness, or she could forget it and just get on with her life.

Maybe he'd moved on, there was nothing there for him now. His church was gone, his accommodation. He was probably on the highway a hundred kilometres away by now. She made herself a cup of coffee, and sat down to think.

At a quarter to twelve the phone rang. It made her jump, and she very nearly didn't answer it. She was feeling very fragile at that moment, and didn't really feel like contact with other people. When she picked it up she was surprised to hear Richard's voice.

'Brindy, are you all right? I was looking for you last night and I couldn't find you anywhere.'

'Yes, Richard, I'm all right. But you were right about one thing – that Pastor was a scumbag. I'll tell you all about it one day.'

'Well, what I phoned for, there's a body over at Valhalla, just come in. James said that if I saw you, would I pass the message on. He needs a make-over doing, fairly urgent.'

Brindy pulled a face. It was really the last thing she felt like doing today.

'Isn't there anyone else available, Richard? I had a bloody awful night, and I was going to give today a miss.'

'James has already covered the other bases. He needs you, Brindy. It's up to you of course, but he would really appreciate it.'

Brindy sighed. No peace for the wicked, she thought.

'Okay Richard. You've twisted my arm. I'll be half an hour.'

Richard put the phone down and punched the air. 'Yes!' He had steeled himself for this moment, and now there was no going back. He went to his private drug supply, and took out a phial of white powder. Then he looked out a hypodermic, and placed that in his pocket. Finally, he took some pills out of the cupboard, and pocketed them. No sense in not being prepared for every eventuality.

Walking across the cemetery towards Valhalla, he thought he could hear a thumping sound, and a low call for help; but even though he stopped and listened, the sound didn't come again. He thought he must have been imagining things.

James was in his office when Richard got there, and Richard pulled the door to. 'She's coming, James. I'm going to need your help.'

'Who's coming? What are you on about.'

'Brindy. Remember our agreement? Well, she's coming over now. I've told her that you have a new cadaver to be made up. It will seem natural if you meet her here. Tell her there's been a bit of a hold-up, and offer her a coffee while she waits. Put two of these in and she'll be asleep in two minutes.'

'Now hang on a minute, doctor. I don't know whether I want to be this closely involved. After all, we've already had an attempt on Augusta's life, and that all went pear-shaped. Agnes is up there, right now, paralyzed!'

'You promised, James. And I'll keep my end of the bargain over this Euthanasia issue. This might be my last chance.'

James shook his head, but reached for the tablets anyway. He frowned, and pushed a lock of hair out of his eyes.

'Okay, you'd better make yourself scarce. Give it enough time to work.'

When Brindy came in, James motioned her to take a seat.

'We've got a last minute hitch, take about twenty minutes to fix. Would you like a coffee while you wait?'

Brindy shook her head.

'No thanks, I just had one at home. I'll have a cold drink though, if you've got one.'

James went out and came back three minutes later with a coke in a glass. He'd had to pound the pills back to a powder form to get them to dissolve. As he sat down, she took a sip.

'I hear that you might be leaving us shortly, Brindy. A little bird told me that you have a major health problem.' James looked at her with hooded eyes.

'You've been talking to Richard. Look, I haven't told anyone, because I'm convinced that I can beat it. He says it's inoperable, and that it's malefic. But I've been trying a theory of my own, and my vision is okay again, and the headaches are gone. I had a slight balance problem too, but that seems to have gone as well. To be honest, I think I've got it beat.'

'Did you tell Dr. Carstairs this,' said James, suspiciously.

'Yes, I've told him ten times if I've told him once. He just can't see any solutions other than medical ones.' She tipped half the drink down her throat. 'I suppose that's only to be expected – that was the way he was trained.'

'Well, I hope you're right,' said James, eyeing her carefully. What was Richard playing at? He hadn't told him all this, only that she was a certainty to die within the next three months. In view of what they were doing, he hoped he was right.

Brindy suddenly dropped her glass on the floor. She slumped in her chair, then shook her head.

'Oh! I'm sorry. I don't know what came over me. God, I feel tired.' The next thing she was out like a light.

Carstairs walked in two minutes later, walked over to Brindy and lifted one eyelid. The pupil was up in her head.

'She'll do. That gives me a couple of hours. I've got a trolley outside. We'll take her to the embalming room.'

'Now hang on, Carstairs. She just told me that she thinks she's got it beat. She says the headaches are gone, and the vision problem.'

Richard shook his head, and clicked his tongue, deprecatingly.

'She's dreaming, James. It's wishful thinking. I tell you that tumour is the most aggressive tumour I've ever seen. It's literally getting ready to swallow the cortex. She could be paralyzed or mad in a week.'

'I hope you're right,' said James. 'I just hope you're right!'

In the embalming room, Richard laid her on the slab, and once he was ready to start, James took off. 'Tell me when it's all over,' he said.

Richard opened the femoral vein first, inserted the tube and watched the first of Brindy's lifesblood start to seep away. He saw her stir at this point, so strapped her arms and legs down, just in case she should wake up and cause a fuss. He was careful as he didn't want to mark her precious skin. He was just about to puncture the carotid artery, when she woke up. She looked down at her bonds, and screamed.

'Hush, hush, it won't take long my sweet, and I'll have you safe at home.'

'Are you fucking mad, Richard? Let me go, this instant.'

'Don't stress yourself. If you strain at those straps you might bruise the flesh. I want you looking beautiful forever.'

'I want me alive, you bastard. What gives you the right to do this to another human being? It's not your life, it's mine, and it might not be much but I want every day of it.'

'But I'm a doctor, Brindy. You don't seem to realize! We sometimes have to make decisions for you, because due to ignorance, or an inability to understand, you're not really competent to make those decisions. That's what we're trained for.'

He made an incision in the carotid artery, and inserted the tube from the formaldehyde pump. Brindy screamed.

'You're not a doctor, you're Frankenstein. You're so full of your own shit that you think you're superior to everyone else. Well it might surprise you to know that other people have ideas and thoughts and wants and desires, and they have intelligence, and they're capable of making their own decisions. They don't need a doctor to make decisions for them.'

'I'm sorry Brindy. But you're too beautiful to let go like this. I'm saving you for a more glorious future, can't you see that? For years of giving others great delight in your loveliness. You'll thank me in the end.'

'How will that be, you Fuck? I'll be dead! Dead!'

Richard pushed the plunger on the formaldehyde pump, and the first of the fluid flowed into her artery. Brindy felt a coldness at her throat, spreading down her side as the liquid advanced.

'Stop, Richard, stop! This is murder. Oh, God, Richard,' she moaned. The pain was suddenly unbearable. She began to go numb, her stomach turned to ice, her chest heaved.

'God help you, Richard! You will be in hell... before... me!' she gurgled.

Suddenly she couldn't speak. She felt the coldness of death running up into her brain, spreading its cold tentacles through her memories as they were erased one by one. The formaldehyde forced its way into every capillary, closing down her systems and driving her blood before it. In its train came the night. Her sight began to dim, and Richard wavered in front of her eyes as someone finally turned the brightness down to zero.

III

Joanne sat at the desk in the little room, and stared at the empty drawer. The letters were gone! How could that be? She'd returned them to their place on the previous visit, and shut the drawer. She'd only pocketed the two letters that she'd read concerning Randolph. She stamped her foot on the floor. Stupid!

The one big chance she'd had, and she'd blown it. Whoever belonged to those footsteps had entered the office and taken the letters while she wasn't around. She was flaming mad, and she stomped out of the office and along the passageway, determined to catch up with whoever it was haunting the old wing and have it out with them.

She went into the ballroom and looked around. Anyone walking from north to south in the South Wing would have to eventually pass through the ballroom, unless they walked along the outside of the building. It was as good a place to start as any. The only problem was that it was so open. There was nowhere to hide in that vast expanse, unless she pulled out that old bureau against the south wall, and hid behind that.

She inspected it more closely. It was fairly large, and had been there for donkeys' years. Whether she'd be able to move it on her own it was hard to tell. She gave it a tentative shove. It was solid, and wouldn't budge. Maybe if she tried picking it up at one end and shoving at the same time. Success this time, it moved a few inches away from the wall. Successive attempts got it far enough out to look behind it, and she could see some sort of square panel, latched against the wall.

It took twenty minutes of lifting and heaving, but she eventually achieved her goal. She got down to try the latch on the panel, and found that it was hinged. It swung out and up.

'Perhaps I can help, young lady!'

Joanne almost jumped out of her skin. She'd heard no one approach, and now she scrambled back onto her feet to find old Frederick standing there, smiling.

'I wondered how long it would take you to stumble across that,' he said. 'It was only a question of time."

'Have you been watching me, Frederick? I've heard footsteps in this wing for the past few days. Was that you?'

'Yes, I must confess, I wondered why this old building held such a fascination for you. You seemed to spend every off duty minute exploring the old place, so I've been keeping an eye on you. Would you care to explain?'

Joanne looked sheepish. 'Oh, well, I suppose it had to come out in the end. I have a personal interest in the old Coverleigh estate, Frederick. You see, my great grandmother was a lady called Margaret Chapland, and she had an affair with Randolph Coverleigh, the one that disappeared. I can't prove it, but I think I'm directly descended from Randolph.'

Frederick took a pace back, and looked at her with new eyes.

'Well, madam. That is an interesting story. And what would your mother's dear name have been, if you don't mind me asking?'

'Her name was Mercy, Mercy Gascon. She married my father, Charles Destry in about 1970. I was born in 1974.'

'And how is your dear mother,' Frederick said, warily.

'She died when I was six. Pneumonia. I don't remember much about her. My father died last year.'

'So what makes you think you are linked to the Coverleighs?'

'Well like I say, Margaret Chapland had an affair with Randolph before he disappeared in 1928. It was always rumoured that she was pregnant to him, but it was hushed up. I found a letter the other day that proves there was a child.'

'Can I see it?'

Joanne pulled the letter out of her pocket, and handed it over. 'I don't think that leaves much room for doubt.'

Frederick took the letter and read it.

'No, it doesn't. There certainly was a child.'

Joanne put the letter away. 'I'm not going to stop until I solve this mystery. I need to know what happened to the child.'

Frederick cleared his throat.

'I think I can be of some help there,' he said.

Joanne looked at him.

'You know? Of course, you've been around here for years, you probably would know. What was the child's name?'

'Oh, I know that as well as I know my own,' laughed Frederick. 'His name was Frederick, Frederick Varley, and he was born in September 1928.'

'Which would make him – seventy-three,' said Joanne, faltering.

'That's right, seventy-three! I'm your grandfather, Joanne.'

IV

There was a good minute or so of total confusion, while Joanne stamped her foot, exploded with a whole collection of why's, how's, when's and wherefore's before throwing her arms around him and giving the old gentleman a hug.

'Please explain - I don't understand. Why Varley. Your mother's name was Chapland. Surely you would have taken your mother's name.'

'My mother's birth name,' chuckled Frederick. 'She was a Varley before she was a Chapland. You see, my mother was born to John Varley and Lydia Chepstow. They were married in 1904, and they had Margaret in 1907. When the First World War broke out, my grandfather lost a pile in stocks and shares, and shot himself. Lydia Varley was left a widow, and in 1917 she married Henry Chapland, the owner of a racing stables. She went to live at Berimma Point, and Margaret, then ten years old, was prevailed upon to adopt her step-father's name, Chapland.'

'When Randolph seemingly left her in the lurch, due, she thought, to her stepfather's interference, she named the child - *me* - Varley. This was too much for Henry to bear, and he banished Margaret from his house. She in turn found it extremely difficult in those days, with no income of her own to support us, and none of the social security support we have today. So she approached the butler of the Great Hall, and arranged for me to be brought up as his child. His wife was childless, and I suppose they derived a great deal of pleasure from having me around the house. The one stipulation was that no one in the house was to be told of my true parentage, for obvious reasons, of course. My true father's name was never mentioned in those days.'

'That must have been very difficult for you,' said Joanne, rubbing his arm.

'Not at all, actually. I wasn't aware of the situation all through my childhood. My mother, Margaret, had gone back to live at Berimma Point, and eventually married a Paul Cannon. They never had any children, for one reason or another. I did see her though.

The butler and his wife would take me for rides into the country, or down to the beach, and once there this mysterious auntie would turn up and show me all sorts of attention. Auntie Mag I used to call her. She never let on that she was my real mother of course, she was too much of a lady for that. I retain a very affectionate regard for her.'

Frederick smiled gently in remembrance, and Joanne gave him a moment for his memories.

'Well, how come I never got to meet you. I could never understand that.'

'Hold on,' Frederick laughed, 'you go too quickly. I grew up, as I said, in the Great Hall, not as the rightful heir, as I should have been, but as the butler's son. My surname in those days was Johns, Frederick Johns. There was nothing to indicate to me that I should have held any higher station than my adoptive father, that of butler. Not until much later, anyway.'

'I left home in 1949, looking to make my way in the world, and I met your grandmother, Olive Gascon. I was only 21, she was sixteen – though she told me she was two years older. One thing led to another, and she became pregnant with your mother, Mercy. She was born Mercy Gascon, because we weren't yet married. That's the name that appeared on her birth certificate. Within a year, your grandmother had run off with a plasterer, Raymond Hunt, and she took Mercy with her.'

'I only saw Mercy occasionally as she was growing up, and when she died, in 1980, I was devastated. But life goes on. I had gone back to the Great Hall during my stepfather's final illness in 1950. When he died in 1951, I was asked if I would take over his role in running the house, the advantage of which was that my stepmother would also be allowed to stay on. So I said yes. I've been here ever since.'

Joanne shook her head. So much detail to remember.

'On my father's deathbed in 1951, he gave me an old, faded envelope, with a statement in it from my natural mother. That supplies all the details you are looking for to prove your connection with the family. It specifically names me as the son of Randolph Coverleigh and Margaret Varley/Chapland, and details her arrangement with the Johns family as to my upbringing. So you can see, there is no mistake. I am your grandfather, and you are a Coverleigh.'

'But, why didn't you ever claim? I can't understand it. You knew in 1951, you had the proof, and Eliza died in 1971. Surely you could have claimed then. You would have had prior claim over Augusta.'

'That's very true, but you must understand that I had been brought up by a servant, and instilled with the manners of a servant. For me to suddenly become the big landholder would have meant a shift in thinking that I was not prepared to contemplate. Besides, I was happy in my position, and by 1971 I had been in that position for twenty years. I preferred to let sleeping dogs lie.'

'But hasn't it galled you, Augusta's arrogance over the years, her intolerance and selfishness.'

'You must realize, Joanne, that Augusta and I grew up together in the Great Hall, she with all the expectations of an heiress, me with none. But we were playmates together, and I grew fond of her, despite her tempers and tantrums. I also recognized that we both came from unstable stock – our grandfather, after all, was Sebastian Coverleigh, who ended his days in an asylum. I could see the instability there, and felt that it would be better if I were to provide a support for her in this life, rather than humble her in the dust. So I chose my own path.'

'You are a very good man, Frederick,' said Joanne, touched by this. 'I'm proud that you're my grandfather.'

'That makes me feel very humble,' said Frederick.

Chapter Seventeen

Adam Cain lay freezing on top of a coffin, and shook as if he had the ague. It was pitch black in there, and he'd found no way of getting out. Unless there was a sudden death in the Varley family, he thought that maybe his time had come. The cold in those marble vaults once the sun went down was bone chilling. He'd been locked in now for about twenty hours, and was hungry, thirsty and frozen to the bone.

At first he'd tried kicking at the doors, then putting his ample shoulder to them, but they were designed to deter people, not encourage them. Without an axe, he had absolutely no show of getting through them. So he'd shouted, called for help until he was exhausted, and his throat was too dry to call any more. He'd investigated the marble slab at the back, which slid out of the way by pulling on a counter-weight. But the counter-weight was outside, no provision had been made for corpses that got up and walked.

As time went on, the level of terror increased. Why had he thought it such a good idea to frighten Brindy Somers. Egged on by Eugenia, he'd let his power go to his head, and now Eugenia was dead, and he was locked in. In the darkness he went back in his mind through the events of his career, and all of a sudden he didn't feel so proud, untouchable and arrogant. He was just human, not a very good human at that, who lived on the sensual plane and encouraged others to do the same. He'd had a good run, but it looked as if the end had come. The only person who would think of looking for him in here was Brindy, and it was doubtful if she'd ever come back, after what he'd put her through.

He was tempted to pray, to ask for forgiveness and a second chance. It even crossed his mind to promise total reform, even celibacy, if God would just once, come to his aid. But even he, with all his bluster, couldn't bring himself to do it. He saw his own hypocrisy even as he considered it, and knew that God wouldn't be fooled for a moment.

He called himself Pastor, and he defiled God. He was headed for hellfire, and there wasn't anything he could do about it.

But perhaps there were worse things than hellfire. In the darkness he heard mutterings, then snufflings, and a scraping of tiny feet on wooden surfaces. There was a scurrying around the outside of the walls, and his hair stood on end as he prepared to face an onslaught in the dark. When it came he screamed and hit out at the little bodies, fighting each other to get at him, ripe flesh, to tear at and feed on. He jumped up and kicked and shouted, and they ran up his legs, biting and gnawing wherever they could get a grip. They ran up his back and bit him on the neck, up his front and bit him on the face.

He exhausted himself with his terror and pain, and fell, only to be engulfed in a sea of tiny bodies tearing at him in the dark. Finally, in desperation, he climbed into the coffin so recently vacated by Brindy, and pulled the lid down over himself. It jammed shut, and although it kept the rats away from his body, his face sat exposed in the circle he'd cut out for Brindy to breathe. In ten minutes Adam had no face at all. They stripped the flesh like a ripe peach, and left him to his dying screams, a bare skull showing through the hole in the lid.

II

Agnes lay, still looking at herself in the suspended mirror. If she could only move, even her hands, it wouldn't be quite so bad. But she was rapidly coming to the conclusion that she would be better off dead. How could she communicate that fact to James, or even Augusta. It looked now as if Augusta was determined to save her, though why, she could not understand. Agnes had tried to murder her, and in the way of poetic justice it had rebounded on her, and put her in this untenable position. All her hopes for the future had died, while Laurens and James still went about their business as usual, untouched by events.

If she could have stamped her foot, she would have done. She concentrated and screwed her eyes shut, and mentally tried to slam her foot against the bottom of the coffin. Nothing! Well, what did she expect? Then she realized that there had been something. She had screwed up her eyes, and in doing so had felt the crinkles across the top of her nose. She tried it again. Yes, she could feel it. Only a tiny area, but she could feel something for the first time in days.

After that a warm area began to extend from her nose around her left eye and down to her cheek. The spot grew wider, and within half an hour she could feel both cheeks, and had a numb sensation in her top lip, as if she'd just had a visit to the dentist. She started to become excited.

'Dear God, keep it happening. Please, dear God, let me recover from this terrible thing.'

She fell asleep later on in the day, and when she woke up she had pins and needles in her left foot. The numb sensation had already extended up to her left knee before she felt a similar sensation in her right foot. Her face was almost back to normal, and she lay pulling faces at herself in the mirror, exercising the muscles, though she couldn't speak as yet.

She slept fitfully that night, a deep growing excitement in her, and when she awoke at two in the morning, her left arm was at the pins and needles stage.

By the next morning she could feel both arms and legs, and most of her body, though there was still a numbness around her stomach and her breasts. But she could rock from side to side in the coffin, and move her arms slightly. She was hoping that someone would show up, Augusta or James, see the improvement and get her out of there. But no-one showed. All she could hear was Gabriel downstairs, playing his medley of hymns and psalms, and she swore then and there that if heaven were like that, she wouldn't be going - ever!

The next few hours were the most frustrating she could ever remember. At eleven o'clock she could just manage a weak squawk, so she squawked and squawked. But no one came. At one in the afternoon a visitor, looking for someone else, saw her lying there and shoved his hand up under her gown. She raised her left leg, put it in the middle of his chest and heaved with all her might. He went flying back and hit the barrier, collapsing onto the floor. When he jumped up he was cursing.

'I'm going to report you. That's not the treatment you expect to get in heaven,' he said, outraged. She put two fingers up and blew a raspberry, and he staggered off, muttering to himself.

At four o'clock someone finally turned up to check her out.

'Get me out of here,' she croaked, much to the assistant's surprise. He had no idea that there was a live one up there, he'd been off for a week and hadn't been briefed.

Thinking that here at last was proof of the resurrection, he helped her out of the coffin and walked her back, yelling 'Glory Hallelujah' as they came down in the lift.

Agnes managed a weak smile as a couple of test corpses on level one sat up and clapped.

III

Richard arranged Brindy in a wicker chair facing his back garden, and stood back to admire his handiwork. He had brushed her hair the way she liked it, and very tediously applied nail varnish to her nails. He realized that he might have to cut them as time went on, as nails and hair tended to continue growing for quite some time after death. But she looked as beautiful as she had in life, only with a quietness about her that she had never, in all honesty, possessed.

He bustled about making breakfast, talking to her as he did so, as if she were sitting waiting for the coffee, but abstracted by something in the garden.

'I don't mind you not talking, darling. I know this is your quiet time of the day. I do enough talking for both of us, don't I? You always used to say that, didn't you?'

He brought toast and two steaming mugs of coffee over to the table, and sat on the other side to her, watching her out of the corner of his eye.

'Now if you move, I'll know straight away. So you just sit perfectly still and we'll enjoy this glorious morning together.'

He drank his coffee and helped himself to the toast, but Brindy just sat there, oblivious to everything.

'Not hungry this morning, dear? It's probably just a touch of a cold. You'll be all right. Are you going to drink your coffee?' When there was no answer he said: 'Oh well, waste not, want not,' and swapped his empty cup for her full one.

'I'll have to go to the surgery later, dear, but I don't want you going anywhere while I'm out. You're too fragile at the moment after that big operation. You need to recuperate. In fact, I think you can have a little sleep while I'm gone, and get up again this evening, watch a bit of telly.'

He went into the bedroom and prepared the bed so he could put her straight in. Then he went back to the lounge and picked her up to carry her back to bed. She just flopped in his arms.

'Hold yourself a bit tighter, dear. It makes it very hard to carry you if you just flop all over the place. Here, I'll tuck you in.'

He placed her in the bed, and was going to cover her up when he had an idea. He pulled her gown up to her waist, stood back and admired her from the foot of the bed.

'Now you be a good girl, and don't go showing that to just anyone, will you,' he said, as he left for the surgery.

Brindy lay exposed and lifeless, and made no comment at all.

IV

'Now you sit down here with me, and I'll make you comfortable,' said Augusta.

She wrapped a shawl around Agnes' shoulders, and generally fussed about her as if there was no tomorrow.

'I'll get you some extra cushions if you want, dear,' she said, caringly.

'Please don't go to all this fuss, Augusta. I know what I did, and I'm sure that when you think about it you'll never be able to trust me again. And who could blame you?'

'Enough of that, Agnes. If it takes something like this to knock some sense into our thick heads, then maybe it was all for the best. By the look of you, you'll make a full recovery, and I thank God for that. If only I had seen the light years ago, but I was so full of myself, Agnes, and so cold and cruel towards everyone else's feelings that I wasn't capable of seeing the damage I was doing.'

'I wish you wouldn't blame yourself so much. We were just as much to blame, wanting things that weren't ours to have. I'm just thankful that you're going to let me stay, Augusta, though I know I don't deserve it.'

'Piffle, woman. From now on you have as much say around here as me. We'll plan everything together, and we might even open up the old South wing again, and throw a few parties. It's been a long time since people laughed and danced under this roof.'

'Oh, do you mean it? That would be marvellous! It was so gay in the old days. Even as a child I remember how gay it used to be.'

'I don't think they use that word in the old sense anymore, Agnes. But you're right, it was cheerful and happy, and we had lots of friends in those days.'

Agnes sat basking in the light of Augusta's new-found devotion, and wiggled her toes every so often just to make sure everything was still intact.

'My only worry at the moment, is James. How do you think he is going to react to a revamped household,' said Augusta. 'I know that there has been no love lost between us in the past, and really, he is the one I find hardest to get along with. What do you think I should do to gain his loyalty, if not his affection.'

Agnes was not used to being consulted on such issues, and got a bit flustered in case she made a whopping fau pas.

'If you want my candid opinion,' said Agnes, trying to sound intelligent, 'the best thing you could do for him would be to sign over Valhalla as a fully fledged concern to him. After all, he might not have paid for it, but he did do all the work.'

Augusta nodded her head.

'I think you might be right, - (she resisted saying 'for once') - Agnes. I think that would show him that I mean business, and it would make him totally independent of us all. Good idea! A young man needs a challenge. He also needs self-respect. That would sort both problems out in one go.'

Agnes sat back as a warm glow flushed over her. She had been accepted as a woman of wisdom at last, and a piece of her advice was going to be acted upon. She sent up silent messages to God all night, thanking him for his favour.

V

Joanne pointed to the latched panel, and Frederick nodded.

'Do you know where it leads?' said Joanne.

'I was afraid you were going to ask me that. Yes, I know where it leads. Mind you, I haven't known for that long, only a matter of months. I came upon it much as you have, by painstaking research and studying old maps.'

'So you've seen the old maps. You didn't by any chance pick up some letters yesterday out of that drawer in the study?'

'I did! I didn't know what you wanted with them at the time, and of course, they are family things, only of interest to us.'

'That's all right then. Are you going to show me what's down the tunnel?'

'Only if you have a strong stomach. Do you? I don't want to upset you.'

Joanne looked at him defiantly.

'I'm pretty tough, and I've come this far.'

'True!' He pulled a flashlight out of his pocket. 'Without one of these, you won't get very far. The tunnels are the remains of old mine shafts. This area was quite rich in copper at one stage, and it was quite close to the surface too. The tunnels followed a reef, though most of them were blocked off years ago for safety. We had a few cave-ins, and that's always a problem.'

They crawled through the panel and slid down a pile of rubble about twenty five feet high. Standing at the bottom, Frederick played his torch around.

'Was there one in 1928,' Joanne asked, following him.

'How very perceptive of you! You've really done your homework, haven't you? Come on, and I'll show you.'

He led her along the tunnel until they came to a three way junction, then turned left. Thirty yards along, the tunnel was blocked by a fall, and Frederick pointed his torch up to the top right, to reveal the bottom of a door.

'That door is in a passageway south of the ballroom. It was supposed to be blocked off years ago, but no one bothered, because the South wing was closed.'

'I found that doorway yesterday,' Joanne said. 'In fact a very distressed man came out of it.'

'Not Dr. Carstairs by any chance? I know! I followed him along until I was sure he was going to get out all right.'

Joanne laughed.

'Is there anything you *don't* know about?'

'Not much around here. I have the advantage of being the walking background. No one notices a butler once he's been around for a while.'

They set off in the other direction, crossing the junction, and heading, Joanne judged, northwest. "

'This tunnel actually passes under the eastern side of the cemetery. In places you can actually see the bottoms of wooden coffins in the roof, where the earth has fallen away.'

Frederick picked out a couple of these spots, and it was quite eerie. In one place a coffin had fallen right through, split open when it hit and scattered the cadaver's bones across the ground. The square shape where the coffin had been was still impressed in the earth above. They kept walking, and the tunnel narrowed for about twenty metres, then widened out into a large cavern. The tunnel continued on the other side of the cavern, but there was something jammed in the opening.

'Here lies the mystery,' said Frederick. 'As his great grand-daughter you should be attuned to the pathos of the scene.'

He stood aside, and shone his light at the other entrance.

It took Joanne a few moments to adjust her eyes to the light, but when she did she took her breath in, sharply. Jammed in the narrow entrance was the remains of a man, still on horseback, though the horse had stumbled to its knees at the front, and was impaled with a long steel spike. The flesh had gone from the bones, but it was unmistakably a horse. The man was dressed in the ragged remains of a red coat, and his neck had been broken somehow, probably by hitting his head on the roof at full gallop.

He sat forward on the horse's withers as it was angled down, and lay leaning backwards in the saddle, his head leaning off at an acute angle. The flesh had rotted off both horse and master, but they had stayed together where they stopped, in an extreme hurry by the look of it. The bones still held together, though they looked as if one good nudge would collapse the entire pile.

'I have refrained from touching my father's body, out of deference to him as a man who *didn't* break his word to a lady after all. From what I can make out, the cave-in occurred the day before, and was on the south side of the South wing. He couldn't see it until he rounded the building on horseback, and was on top of it before he knew it. Both horse and master fell, say thirty to forty feet to the tunnel. Picked themselves up, and madly went exploring. Instead of walking the horse, Randolph spurred it into a gallop, and 'tally-hoed' his way through the tunnels. Perhaps the rest of the cave-in happened then, cutting off his retreat. It is known that hoof-beats were heard under the ballroom for some time after his disappearance. After some days, and almost giving up any thought of being rescued, he galloped back along the tunnel until the horse impaled itself on the steel bar, as you can see, reared in doing so, and hit Randolph's head against the roof, breaking his neck. A poetic end for a poetic man.'

'Randolph,' Joanne breathed, over-awed by the discovery. 'Unbelievable.'

'Welcome to the family, Joanne.'

Chapter Eighteen

James stood up on a gantry, watching the gradually changing face of 'HELL'. There was a small Dodgem circuit below him, where cars driven by cadavers crashed into each other to the sound of riotous laughter through the loudspeakers. He noticed that a couple of unrestrained arms had been amputated during the action, and were lying on the floor, being skidded around by the action of the cars. No doubt the engineers would design a more encompassing safety belt for loose colliding cadavers.

Along the walls were the pokie degenerates, lying in their mobile coffins, which motored out to a poker machine automatically on a rotational basis. Once there the cadaver raised one arm and poked a finger down onto the button. It had been noticed that the flesh on the end of the finger didn't last very long with this repetitive activity, so the bone was showing in a lot of cases. But there had been some talk of a new fingerstall to avoid this problem.

A line of coffins sat in front of a big screen TV, and the cadavers sat up, staring sightlessly at a round of Game Shows from twenty years before. Each time there was a winner, they all mindlessly clapped.

Oh yes, 'HELL' was one big fun parlour of entertainment.

But James wasn't happy. He felt that the way it had been laid out before, with equal sections for 'HEAVEN', 'HELL' and 'PURGATORY' was much more tasteful, and followed the biblical teachings more than this new layout. He knew there had to be progress, but he was a traditionalist at heart and it worried him now to see his metronome cast aside, pushed against a rear wall where it could no longer tick off the seconds of man's sins, or the message that 'time waits for no man.'

With 'HELL' taking over popular culture the way it had done, man had nothing *but* time. Eternity to re-visit the sins of his youth! Heaven had shrivelled to a small area full of anally retentive corpses, trying desperately to uphold outmoded ideas from the 19th century. From James' point of view, it was a tragedy. But it was good marketing!

Meanwhile, Werner von Keppler sat in his lounge room, watching a continuous display of adverts for the new-style Valhalla. The more he saw, the more disgusted he became, and 'Gott in

Himmel', 'Vucking Bulls-Chit', and 'Vuncken' Hell!' were remarks that he illustrated the ads with. He sat up late at night and perfected his mercury switch, then attached it to a bundle of high explosive and an alarm clock. He had plans of his own.

II

Richard came home from work, expecting Brindy to be waiting at the door with a welcoming kiss. She wasn't. When he finally found her, she was lying on the bed, exposing herself in the most shameless way. He had no idea that Brindy was capable of this sort of behaviour, and was shocked.

'I really think there's a time and a place for that sort of thing, Brindy. I'm disgusted at you,' he said, adjusting her gown so she would appear modest. He shook his head, disbelievingly.

'I had no idea that you were that sort of a girl, Brindy. I thought you had taste and style. What if one of the neighbors had called in for a cup of sugar? Would you have gone to the door like that? I find it hard to understand.'

He went out of the bedroom and into the lounge, talking through the door.

'Have you been in bed all this time, Brindy. I know I said to have a sleep, but I did think you'd be up by this. What's the matter – cat got your tongue or something?'

He went in and carried her out, and sat her up at the dining table. She kept slumping over, and once she totally fell off her chair.

Richard snorted in disgust.

'For God's sake, Brindy, pull yourself together! I've got enough to do without picking up after you all night. Now sit up straight in your chair, and pay attention. There's going to be a few rules instituted around here, and you're going to listen.'

Brindy stared at the table, watching her arm slowly sliding out from under her. Her nose flattened on the surface, and Richard yanked her back up by the hair.

'Sit straight, I said,' he yelled, 'and pay attention.'

He paced up and down, trying to make sense of his muddled thoughts..

'Now a joke's a joke, and I can take a joke as well as the next man. But if you're going to continue to cut me out of your life, Brindy, you and I are going to fall out.'

Brindy stared at him, her features beautiful but motionless.

'You're going to have to put a bit more effort into this relationship, Brindy. I can't carry it all on my own.'

He turned on the television as an ad for Valhalla was showing.

'Is your partner over the hill? Do you ever think that a change might be nice? If YOUR partner conforms with the following criteria, then we might be able to help. If he or she is (a) Dead; (b) Dying; (c) Is always saying they'd rather be dead; (d) has attempted suicide in the past; (e) has a terminal illness; (f) thinks they have a terminal illness, but hasn't; (f) is in favour of Euthanasia; (g) thinks that life is good, but death is better - then we can definitely help! There are limited vacancies at Valhalla this month for all the above categories. Remember, Valhalla brings death to life!'

'Did you see that Brindy. I sometimes wonder if that's what you'd prefer. Would you, Brindy? I know that it must be boring, stuck with a doctor, but it was your choice, remember. You wanted me to get rid of your tumour, didn't you? Well, I got rid of it, didn't I. Your tumour will never worry you again.'

He suddenly sat down, and covered his face.

'That's it, isn't it Brindy. Even in death, that tumour is eating away at your brain. Even now, it's affecting your speech, confusing your thinking. Good God, what was I thinking of? We've got to get rid of that tumour, Brindy. We've got to excise it from your body, or it will keep growing, it will eventually burst out and cover your entire body. It will eat all that beautiful flesh. Don't worry my darling. I'll operate tonight. We'll get rid of that tumour once and for all. Then you'll be free of it, my dear. Then we can settle down and be happy together. Just one more operation, Brindy, and no blood, I swear, there'll be no blood.'

III

'So it's finally been revealed to us, after all these years.'

Augusta spoke, and looked musingly at Frederick and Joanne across the dining table. Agnes sat next to her, and shook her head, as if not believing what she was hearing.

'But you can't do anything about it now,' said Agnes, jumping to Augusta's defence. 'It's too late, years too late.'

'I always thought my parents knew more than they were saying,' said Augusta. 'That would have been my mother. She never had any time for her brother, Randolph.'

'Don't worry, Agnes. If I was going to do anything about it, I would have done it in 1951, or 1971 at the latest.' Frederick was saying, to put Agnes at rest.

'Why didn't you, Frederick? After all, you were cheated out of your birthright. No one would have blamed you, you know.' Augusta looked sadly at him.

'I preferred things the way they were, madam. I always thought that we were... well... friends.'

'I have always thought so, Frederick. Now I know that you were much more than a friend to me.' Augusta's eyes glistened with tears.

'However, madam, now that my grand-daughter has turned up, I would expect that she be recognized when the time comes.'

'Only fair, Frederick! She will be. I give you my word on that, my dear. In the meantime you will both make your home with us, in this house, and no more having to act like paid employees.'

'Thank you,' said Joanne, blushing. 'I'm just sorry that I had to go about it in such an underhanded way, that's all.'

'Hah! Underhanded! That's the way this entire family has operated ever since I can remember. It just proves you are one of us.'

They all laughed.

IV

James called in two of the Valkyrie the following morning. He had a special assignment for them. It was all very well trusting underlings with first priority business, but in the end, if you wanted something doing you had to do it yourself.

He had been watching from a distance since the exhumation of the phantom Indigo Appledean, and it had disturbed him to see the new closeness that seemed to be developing in the family. Augusta was going through some sort of vague repentance for giving everyone thirty years of hell, but she wasn't fooling James. Agnes might sit up in the Great Hall now, reflecting in the glow of approval after totally cocking up the murder plan, but he knew that there was some secret agenda that Augusta was following, and he believed it was tied up with his inheritance.

When he heard via the grapevine that Frederick and Joanne had turned out to be long lost descendants of mad Randolph, then he could wait no longer. Possibly they hadn't got their proof together yet – not enough to stand up in a court of law, anyway – so he needed to move quickly if he wasn't to see his inheritance dissipated between half a dozen claimants. He handed some papers to one of the Valkyrie and explained patiently what he wanted her to do. They left immediately, and headed for the Great Hall.

Augusta was up and about early after checking in on Agnes and seeing her happily engaged in her coffin. She herself had avoided the romper room for the past couple of days, as she had discovered that the real thing was still the best with Laurens returning to the fold, to this new, soft Augusta.

Frederick was not around when the Valkyrie knocked at the great door, so Augusta answered it herself. The girls amused her in their Scandinavian clothes and their Viking helmets, not to mention the plaits, but she listened to what they had to say then graciously bestowed her signature on the form they proffered.

She was at breakfast with Agnes, pushing more toast in her direction, when she mentioned their visit. Frederick was standing in the background, and couldn't help overhearing the conversation.

'I had visitors this morning, Agnes, before you were even up.'

Agnes looked at her over a mouthful of toast.

'Yes. Delightful girls. James has a petition going, and he's using the Valkyrie to go around collecting signatures. So I signed. Just a charity thing, something about 'Youth in Asia'. Well, I've always had a soft spot for youth, when I'm not in a grumpy mood, anyway, and these days it's all multicultural, isn't it.'

Frederick leant over the table and re-filled madam's coffee cup.

'Would you remind repeating that, madam. Perhaps I'll have to look into it myself.'

'Oh, certainly Frederick. 'Youth in Asia.' Something about helping our Chinese friends I think. I'm all for it.'

'I see, madam,' said Frederick, his brow growing black. After breakfast he excused himself, as there were some groceries to be picked up, and a few errands to be run in Port Waterdale. No one saw him for the rest of the day.

Werner von Keppler was at late breakfast when Frederick called in. They had known each other for years, and Frederick enquired about Werner's health, and whether he had participated in any good ballot burning exercises lately. Werner grinned, and they exchanged chit-chat about various existentialist philosophies, and how the nihilist movement was going in outer Bessarabia. Then Frederick came to the point.

'Werner, as you well know, my family name is Varley, we have that large Vault in the cemetery, the dark marble one. It has been neglected over the years, so I popped my head in recently to tidy up, and guess what I found? An intruder, Werner; a cadaver that had squatted in our lot, you might say.'

'Now I have no quarrels with helping people in need. Indeed, I subscribe to the 'Down & Out Magazine'. But I do resent cadavers in the honourable family plot, especially when they haven't been introduced.'

'Who is t'is cadaver? Haf you any idee vot his name iz?'

'None whatever, old fellow. Therein lies the rub. Without a name I cannot return the corpse to its rightful owners, nor indeed get them to accept responsibility for the cost of its re-interment.'

'Can you take picture of itz face, and maybe advertize?'

'It wouldn't do any good, old fellow. It seems this cadaver had a brush with my rat collection, and his face has quite disappeared. You can see the spot I'm in. I don't want to go to the law, because they would be asking awkward questions about why I kept my rats there in the first place.'

'Hey! Vot better place to keep zuh rats, huh? Zees aut'orities, zey haf no humour.'

'Quite right, Werner. Anyway, I wondered if you had any little schemes going on at the moment whereby you would be in need of a cadaver. Remarkably handy things to have on occasion..'

'I see vot you mean! Aha! Now I just might be able to use zis in connection viz a plan I am developing at zis very moment. It comes viz zuh box, Ya?'

'The box? Oh, the coffin... yes Werner. Complete with coffin. Just one thing, however. A circle has been cut out around the face of this one. Not a pretty sight, I can assure you. And there has been no embalming, so its use-by date is rather limited I'm afraid.'

'How long,' said Werner, stroking his chin, ruminatively.

'Two days, tops. You would need to collect it tonight. I shall give you a hand if required.'

'Zat will be all right. Just leave zuh key to zuh vault. I can fix it.'

'I trust you will put it to good use, Werner. Knowing you, I'm sure you will.'

V

Richard sat at the kitchen table, his head in his hands, his hair flying in all directions as if he'd been caught in a great wind. It was dark outside and the air was chill.

Brindy sat in her wicker chair and would have stared at the stars, except that she was minus a head. The head lay on the kitchen table, severed at the neck, and the brain lay in front of it. Richard looked at the cortex, and a tear squeezed out of one eye and down his cheek. The tumour was gone. Not only was the tumour gone, but there was no sign that it had ever existed, though Richard knew full well it had.

There was no question about that. The tumour had been a nasty, invasive and malefic tumour which the best neurosurgeon in the country had declared inoperable. But it had gone. That scumbag Pastor and his nasty little god had done the trick.

Brindy would have lived!

Suddenly the pursuit of medicine attained the proportions of throwing chicken bones in a heap, and divining the future from where they landed. All the scientific sureties had completely disappeared, leaving Richard staggering at the abyss of his own ignorance. The tumour had gone!

Eventually he roused himself, and looked at the head. Then he looked at the body in the chair. He scowled.

'Oh, for God's sake, Brindy. Pull yourself together!'

He put on his hat, and took a last look at his beloved. She would have been beautiful if she'd lived.

'This obviously isn't going to work out, Brindy. You'll be blaming me forever for not listening to you, and I will always resent that preacher you ran off with. I can see it now, argument after argument, and misery for us both.

I think we're going to have to call it quits. Goodbye!'

He left by the front door, and headed for Valhalla. He went in by the visitor's entrance and vaulted a security fence to get through to the embalming room. The few visitors that were there were too busy watching the Dodgems to take any notice of him. He made his way to the embalming room and mixed up a new potion of formaldehyde and water, then heated it to body temperature. No sense in making things any worse than they were already.

Sitting on the slab, he managed to find his femoral vein, nick it and insert the waste tube. His blood began disappearing down the tube into the drain. He made a mental note that he'd have to wash that out once he was finished, or it would end up clogging up. Then with the aid of a mirror, he located his femoral artery and made an incision, sliding the tube from the hand pump into place. With a last look around him, and a muttered 'Brindy', he started to pump like mad.

Within forty-five seconds he was dead.

Chapter Nineteen

James didn't discover the body until the following morning. He stood and stared in disbelief, then stamped on the ground and swore.

'What the bloody hell? Richard! How the hell am I going to get a second signature now?'

Suddenly his scheme had come to nothing. Augusta's signature on the application for Euthanasia was only good with two doctors' signatures to back it. He'd thought he had two, Laurens and Carstairs, both in his pocket. Now it appeared that one had decided to top himself.

He went off to the office to call the police. Let them deal with it. Whatever he'd done it for, he was no use to him now. Then he thought of Brindy. What had he done with Brindy? That question was answered later in the day when Constable Porter turned up, to inform him that Carstairs had a headless corpse in his living room, and a brain lying on the table.

'Looks like he must have gone a bit loopy,' said the policeman. 'He's got her sitting there with coffee spilt all down her front, and donuts shoved in all her orifices,' he said. 'Maybe he was trying to get her to eat, or something. Gee, there's been some queer stuff happening around here lately.'

James nodded his agreement, and wandered off to be some place where he could be on his own. He stood up on the gantry and looked down at 'HELL'. It had taken over his life. 'HEAVEN' and 'PURGATORY' weren't in it.

He looked around and saw the first few corpses going up for their flying lessons. The engineers had come up with some ingenious lightweight wings, and these, aided by huge fans to create an updraft enabled the flyers to glide about above the seventh level, occasionally side-slipping over "PURGATORY' and 'HELL' in their exploratory swoops. This was at least one activity not open to the residents of 'HELL'.

Looking down, James saw a coffin come trundling in through the door, a white-coated assistant sliding it onto the conveyor that would take it to 'HELL'. There was something about the coffin that caused alarm bells to ring in James' mind, the lid was cut out in a circle, and the face showing had been stripped of all its flesh. He wasn't going to have that thing coming in here!

James dashed down the stairwell as the coffin moved off along the conveyor. By the time he got down there the white-coated assistant had disappeared, so James tried to follow the coffin on its journey through the levels. Suddenly it was as if every elevator and every conveyor in the place started up, and began to shuffle coffins from their home base to different positions in the building. James thought for a moment that it might be the day that the coffins were advanced or retarded in their movement towards 'PURGATORY', but then he realized that there was another two weeks before that was scheduled.

He caught sight of the coffin with the skull face, rolling along the seventh level of 'HELL' and jumped on a conveyor himself, determined to track it until it stopped. He'd get to the bottom of this if it killed him.

Each time he got near to it, the coffin would race off in a new direction, or sink two levels before taking off again. James signalled an engineer to stop the works, but the engineer shrugged his shoulders as if to say: 'Can't be done. It's jammed!'

Finally James outsmarted it by climbing up two levels above it, and waiting for it to come around before leaping down and hanging on for grim death. He looked down at the fleshless face, and felt a portent of disaster. There were wires wrapped around the head, visible from the outside. This wasn't just any ordinary corpse.

James rode the coffin like a cowboy, signalling madly to the floor below to either turn off the power, or come up and help, but they just stood and watched him, careering around corners, hanging on for grim death. The coffin took a dive down a lift, then ran around level three. It was going down in its flight through 'HELL'. As it descended to each lower level it seemed to speed up, and it finally hit the floor at thirty miles an hour, spun off the conveyor and into the middle of the Dodgem cars.

With James still riding it rodeo style, the coffin bumped off the various cars and spun across the slippery floor, almost unseating him. He just heard the first stroke of midday chime, and an alarm clock went off in his mobile coffin. Suddenly 'HELL' went up in an explosion that totally destroyed the building, while James vaporized somewhere along with the visitors.

A flame shot a hundred feet into the air as the explosion rocked the town of Port Waterdale. Coffins that moments before had been ranged in front of poker machines flew into people's gardens and bounced off their roofs, the corpses continuing to poke their fingers up and down to chance their luck on the now non-existent buttons.

The strangest phenomenon however, were the five flying cadavers with ultralight wings, who had caught the updraft and headed for the coast before gliding back over the town almost an hour after Valhalla had gone up. It took eight hours to put out the fire, by which time most of the inhabitants had been well and truly cremated. It took twelve hours to get the flying cadavers back to earth, the last two being shot out of the sky by the police helicopter before they caused damage to high voltage power lines.

After the ruins had been reduced to embers, it was seen that the explosion had blown a hole through the floor and into an underground chamber, and most of Valhalla had fallen into that.

Buried somewhere beneath those levels, conveyors, lifts and a giant metronome, were the long dead bones of a man in a red coat, and those of his horse.

II

Port Waterdale has never been the same since. If you should visit the Great Hall you would be met by Joanne Coverleigh, once known as Destry, who inherited the estate from Augusta when she died. Doc Laurens has long since quit the town, and lives in drunken retirement somewhere in Indonesia, where the natives are friendly and the cost of living minimal – except for the price of a bottle of Jim Beam a day. The exchange rate makes that an exhorbitant expense, equivalent to a month's groceries.

Frederick died shortly after Augusta, and is firmly planted in the Varley Vault in the cemetery. It was as if he couldn't continue without her once she died, and followed on swiftly to continue his role as faithful butler to the old tartar. His ghost is said to control a huge collection of rats that maraud through the cemetery and the remaining tunnels below, each night. The local council carries out a regular extermination program, but this has not been greatly successful as they appear to breed so quickly. Thus the forty or so feral cats that inhabit the cemetery grounds are allowed to go free as an added control mechanism.

Agnes spends most of her spare time in her coffin, dreaming weird dreams and staring out of her window at the park outside. When she does occasionally stir herself to go into the world, a small car takes her into town and deposits her outside the religious bookshop, where she buys huge tracts of literature as if in penance. She still eats all the toast at breakfast, and is quite plump and rosy cheeked these days.

Werner von Keppler no longer lives locally, toying with his mad inventions. He is now a permanent inmate of a mental institution, since being apprehended attempting to smuggle a coffin into state parliament through the tradesman's entrance. Once it was established that the coffin contained a corpse armed with an AK-47, Werner was taken into custody and never reappeared. His bed is said to be surrounded by alarm clocks, all in various stages of dismemberment.

Jonathon Pepper finally retired, and lives on the income generated by his pop-ups. Edmund took over the family business, but spends most of his time travelling, and setting up franchises interstate and overseas. He finds the role of high-flying executive far more to his taste than the laying out of corpses.

Brindy Somers lies preserved in a large glass container of formaldehyde, rather like a ship in a bottle. She has pride of place in the exhibits room of the police museum, and delights thousands of sniggering recruits each year with her perfect, headless body.

Nearby, in another bottle, is James Coverleigh's left foot, which was found on the roof of the local hotel after the explosion. No other part of him was ever recovered. The foot was only recognized by the remains of a tell-tale monogrammed sock, and the application of DNA testing.

III

The circumstances of Augusta's death turned out to be the strangest result of the entire affair. After the explosion, a piece of charred paper landed in the grounds of the local hospital, and was picked up by a medical orderly. On scanning its contents he placed it in the in-tray of a visiting locum who was in the habit of signing everything put in front of him, and the paper was then forwarded to the Department of Health.

Noticing the absence of a second signature, an officious clerk then forwarded the form to the senior medical officer in charge of pensions and allowances, where it was intercepted by a junior medical officer just out of university. Wishing to appear efficient, this junior signed his name with a flourish, and dropped it onto the senior's desk.

Noting that the form had been duly signed by two doctors the senior then passed the form in a brand new file cover to the newly created Department of Terminations and Implementation. They assigned the case to the Port Waterdale Hospital Medical Officer, who just happened to be a certain locum at that time as the two resident doctors had suddenly become unavailable; one due to his untimely death, the other due to a windfall of $50,000 which had permitted him to retire.

A letter was formally sent to Augusta Branwood, advising her that she should attend the following week for her medical procedure to be carried out. Thinking that they had finally got around to fitting her in for some minor elective surgery to her arthritic left hand, she duly arrived for her appointment.

On arrival she was wheeled into a private room, given a cup of tea, and asked to sign a consent form. She didn't even bother to read it. By the time her suspicions had begun to rise, the locum was already injecting a lethal dose of some heart stopping liquid into her vein.

'Is this the local anaesthetic, young man,' she demanded.

'You don't need an anaesthetic for this one. Death is fairly instantaneous.'

'Did you say 'Death?''

Augusta was still staring in disbelief when her heart stopped beating. She just caught the locum's feeble joke as her eyes began to glaze over.

'Don't tell me; you just came in to have a corn plaster removed!'

Still grinning, he threw a sheet over Augusta's head, and went off to have lunch.